Voice to Raise

ROAD TO ROCKTOBERFEST 2025

GABBI GREY

Malik

Until I turned twenty-five, I took the safe route, the good boy route. Played with the orchestra, kept my head down, didn't make waves. Now I can't stay silent any longer. I walked away from my violin, relearned the guitar, and started a rock band. With Razor Made, I can create the music I've always dreamed of, and we're good enough to win an invite to Rocktoberfest. But I also love my band for helping me raise my voice to support social justice. Now I just need to convince Spencer I can chase musical success and still be deeply committed to making a difference.

Spencer

I've been fighting for justice practically from the cradle, and I believe organizers should welcome everyone who wants to be involved. That said, when an upstart rock star looking for the limelight comes to join our fight, I'm skeptical. I want true believers, not people who are looking to leverage our cause into a viral hit. Malik might be gorgeous, and even a sweet guy under the tattoos and bad boy persona, but he's chasing his dream of fame in Black Rock while I'm on the ground in Vancouver trying to make meaningful change. He doesn't have room in his life to be serious about music, serious about justice, and serious about me.

Voice to Raise: Rocktoberfest 2025 is an opposites-attract, age-gap, interracial, hurt/comfort gay romance novel about the power of activism, making a commitment, and how chasing one dream can open your heart to another

The boys are back in the multi-author Road to Rocktoberfest 2025 series. Each book can be read as a standalone, but why not read them all and see if some of your past favorites poke their heads in. Err...voices. Hot rock stars, stolen kisses, drywall repairs and the men who drive them over the edge. What more could you ask for? Kick back, load up your e-readers and enjoy the men of Rocktoberfest!

multimedia, audio, or other medium. We support the right of humans to control their artistic works.

No generative AI was used in the creation of this book.

Edits by ELF

Cover by Jo Clement

Dedication

Dave

Renae

Kaje

Wendy

ELF

Contents

Prologue

Malik

I'm finished.

I eased my violin into its case for what I was completely convinced was the last time.

Everyone in the orchestra was packing up, and a lump formed in my throat. I'd been one of the youngest violin players ever—and I was still young. According to Lionel, our conductor, I hadn't even hit my stride. I wasn't yet in my prime. He predicted great things for me.

I saw only drudgery. Doing the same thing over and over again. Certainly, the music would change. We even did some more-progressive pieces. But rarely experimental. Certainly not anything that truly challenged me. I'd been a prodigy and had learned the basics by the age of five. Done my first solo concert at ten. Joined the junior orchestra at twelve.

Now, at twenty-five, I felt all washed up. Disillusioned. Ready for something new.

Charles the cellist approached. "I'm looking forward to next season."

I smiled, even as my chest squeezed. He'd always been so kind to me. "I, uh, won't be here."

He blinked. "I'm sorry?"

"I've tendered my resignation. Tonight was my final concert."

"Are you going elsewhere? I considered Stockholm once—all those blond men." He sighed. "Alas, I'm a Canadian at heart. I was glad to leave Alberta, though. Vancouver is more my speed."

His words resonated. Parts of Alberta—including where he'd come from—weren't gay friendly. Vancouver, on the other hand, had a thriving gay community. When I'd turned nineteen, I'd started exploring the clubs. Had enjoyed a few hookups along the way.

Was still looking for *the one*.

"Vancouver is great." *My hometown.* "But I'm not leaving for another position. I have to—" I swallowed. "I need more. This isn't enough for me."

"You need to fly."

I cocked my head.

He shrugged. "I get it. I really do. For me, that was leaving my small town. Perhaps for you, it's something different."

"Yeah. I've, uh, been playing around with my old guitar. It's acoustic, and that's not really my jam anymore either. I'm thinking about an electric guitar. Maybe...I don't know...rock'n'roll...?"

"Well, that's definitely something completely different. I applaud your bravery. Will you—" He rubbed his forehead. "Will you have enough money?"

As he was well-aware, my parents weren't around anymore. They died four years ago in an automobile crash. At least they'd lived long enough to see my success. In truth, they probably wouldn't have supported my leaving a great job for something as insane as starting a rock band.

"I've landed a job as an assistant at the studio over in East Van. They're big. Some of the biggest names in town record all their albums and rehearse there. The pay's not great, but I own my house." The thing had been paid off when my parents died. "I'm considering renting out the lane house, and I might get a tenant or two to share my place. I've got spare bedrooms. I'm thinking students."

"Ensure you vet them carefully." Charles frowned.

I smiled. "I will. I promise."

His frown didn't lessen. "I'm not going anywhere. I expect regular updates."

"I promise that as well." Charles had been like a second father to me—perhaps even more than my own.

My parents had been older when they had me, and I was an only child. Charles, booted by his biological parents when he was fourteen after having been caught with another boy and refusing to renounce being gay, had made his way to Vancouver. Since he was homeless and alone, social services had put him into foster care with the Wonnocks. They were a boisterous family with many siblings—some of blood and some of love—like Charles. Foster children who'd wound up being adopted as he had. Siblings of those kids. Just a riot of people. Many of those kids were now married, so there were almost as many grandchildren as there were children.

I was often invited to their gatherings. I thought I'd be able to disappear, but I could always count on someone speaking to me. The younger kids loved looking at my tattoos, so I always wore shirts without sleeves to show them off.

All the ink was acquired after my parents passed. They wouldn't have approved.

Charles held his arms open.

I stepped into the embrace. I had about six inches on him—what with me being five-nine. He never complained about how short he was. In fact, he never complained about anything. He was just one of those people who smiled all the time. Truthfully, I wanted to be more like him.

He released me and whistled.

Everyone turned to him.

"You may not have heard that Malik is leaving the orchestra. We all wish him well in his future endeavors, right?"

Another thirty minutes passed before I was able to make my escape—everyone wanted to tell me how much they'd miss me.

I wavered on whether or not doing this was the right thing or not. Giving up stability—and the people who'd cared for me after I lost my parents—felt monumental.

And yet, the time had come.

Charles and I walked out together into the fresh night air. Night had fallen, and Vancouver was illuminated by all the lights.

"Any plans for Canada Day?" He glanced my way.

I shook my head. "I think I'll still be coming to terms with my decision. But I'm working in the studio starting on July third. That'll keep me busy."

"Ah, yes." He squeezed my shoulder. "Be good. Call and write often. We do drinks once a month."

Neither of us were big drinkers, but I understood the sentiment.

Something shifted within me.

This was big.

Huge.

Life-changing.

I just didn't know how things were going to play out. But damn it, I was going to become a rock star.

Chapter One

Spencer

"What do you mean, *Malik Forestal chained himself to the Lion's Gate Bridge?*" I pressed a hand to my forehead. "Who the hell is *Malik Forestal?*"

Bonnie stared at me. "You've never heard of Malik Forestal? Razor Made?"

I stared right back. "Nope. But you had better enlighten me. We blocked the bridge for twenty minutes. We inconvenienced commuters."

"Annoyed the shit out of them."

"Well, that's the point. If they want to drive gas-guzzling vehicles, they can be inconvenienced."

My assistant shook her head. "Right, like them all idling while we held them up didn't contribute to greenhouse gas emissions."

I wrinkled my nose. "We got our point across—we don't need another pipeline."

"You realized Vancouver has a high percentage of drivers who, you know, drive electric vehicles? And our electricity is clean. We want to encourage this. Not make them sit in traffic as well."

"We didn't have a way to separate them." At this hour of the morning, we had two lanes coming from the North Shore into Vancouver and one lane heading the other way. Heavy traffic that wasn't moving fast—hence our ability to step before them and block the road.

To say we weren't popular was an understatement—but we'd effectively made our point. "I know you weren't in favor—"

She cleared her throat.

"Okay, at all supportive—"

She tipped her chin up.

"But we needed to do something. Did you see the press who swarmed?"

"I haven't watched the footage yet. I only just found out about Malik."

"What happened?"

"Blossom said the cops broke the chains and hauled him off to jail."

Again, I pressed my hand to my forehead. I'd been busy dispersing the volunteers who'd helped with the blockade, then making my way back to the office on my bicycle. I'd ignored my phone chirping at me continuously.

Obviously, that'd been a mistake. Perhaps if I'd still been on the bridge, I might've resolved the situation without having to involve the police.

"Was this guy on our list?"

Bonnie shook her head. "Nope. Blossom says she invited him this morning, and he leapt at the chance. I just know about the album he released in the spring."

I blinked. "Album?"

"Yeah, Razor Made's first mainstream release. They've got a few videos up on YouTube. Millions of hits. They parlayed that into a studio album."

"And how do you know all this?"

"Blossom."

"Of course." The woman was our social media guru. Very talented with all things internet. Sometimes, though, she needed to be reined in. I sighed. "Where is Malik now?"

"He's at the cop shop. Blossom's certain he's going to be released without charges."

I wanted to scoff at that, but a few of our other protests had gotten...a little out of hand. Which had resulted in a handful of arrests. A few stern warnings. But as of yet, no actual charges. Not that some of the members of This Land is Ours weren't willing. I did my best to explain repeatedly that running afoul of the law was not the best way to get our message across. Sure, those arrests might get press coverage. Sometimes, though, bad news was just that—bad.

"Is there someone we should be calling?"

Bonnie squinted. "His parents died tragically about five years ago. I suppose I could try one of his bandmates. Like..." She rolled her eyes upward to stare at the popcorn ceiling of the room.

We were headquartered in an old house from the 1920s—a donation to our organization from a fervent environmentalist who never had kids but wanted to leave a legacy.

We hung a photo of Maude Ransom in the front foyer. Of her up an old-growth tree in 1999. When she was 71 years old. She'd lived another twenty-three years, only giving up the ghost in 2022. Chastity had been running This Land Is Ours back then and had gladly taken the house. Lovely woman, clearly over her head. She hadn't understood the ramifications of that decision or what would be involved in keeping a house like this on the organization's books. So when I arrived the next year, the timing was perfect. My legal background fit.

Chastity took off for the Amazon rainforests as soon as she dropped this hot potato into my lap—never to be heard from again.

I wished the authorities in Brazil well—grateful she was someone else's problem. As I'd dug through the org's books for the three years she'd been in charge, I'd found hundreds of errors in our accounting entries and with our tax filings. How we hadn't triggered an audit by the Canada Revenue Agency was beyond me—but we hadn't. It had taken me six solid months of working with an accountant to get everything resolved. During that time, much of our fundraising had been put on hold, and we hadn't done many activities.

In an effort to regain momentum, I hired Bonnie, who recruited Blossom, and now we had a guy in jail.

My headache grew in intensity. "You think you can track down someone?"

Bonnie met my gaze. "Well, they're all on the socials. I can get Blossom—"

"I'd really prefer you do it yourself. You're here, after all. Blossom's not." Whether she would appear was a crapshoot. We weren't paying her, so she kept her own hours. I was grateful that she mostly—mostly—took the direction I gave her.

"Well, Creed's got a ton of followers—"

"Creed?"

She glanced up from her screen, her blue eyes wary at my tone. "I don't think that's his actual name. He doesn't have a last name or anything."

"Of course he doesn't." I waited impatiently as she typed out a message with her thumbs flying across her screen. I, on the other hand, pecked out messages with my right index finger. Predictive text was my best friend. Autocorrect was my archenemy.

"Okay, sent. We'll just—"

Her phone buzzed.

"He's responded. He wants to call."

"Give him my number."

"Okay, but he's going to expect me." Even as she said the words, she typed.

About twelve seconds later, my phone rang. "Spencer Wainright."

"Uh, I thought I was gonna talk to Bonnie. My name's Creed."

"I'm Bonnie's—"

She arched her eyebrow—daring me to announce myself as her boss.

I cleared my throat. "I'm a friend of Bonnie's. We work at This Land Is Ours. Have you heard of us?"

"Sure. Malik talks about you guys all the time. TLIO this and TLIO that. I thought maybe he met a guy who hooked up with him and dragged him, but he said he just felt compelled to get involved."

Met a guy who hooked up with him... Did that mean Malik was gay? Now was precisely not the time to think about that, but I tucked that nugget into the back of my mind. "Uh, we understand he was arrested after the, uh, incident on the Lion's Gate Bridge."

"No shit. He was filming himself when he chained himself. I hadn't heard anything about being arrested."

"Well, I believed it was prudent to inform someone. Apparently, he was the only person taken into custody."

Bonnie nodded vigorously.

"Yeah, that's Malik. Kind of amazing it hasn't happened before now. I suppose I should go down and see if I can bail him out."

"If he's charged, he'll have to go to court first. If he's charged, you might need to secure a lawyer for him."

He chuckled. "No worries—my mother will take care of all of that."

"Excuse me?"

"She's a lawyer. Legal aid. I don't know whether she can represent him, but she'll know what to do. So, like, thanks for letting me know." He paused. "He didn't cause any trouble or anything, did he?"

"He got arrested."

"Wearing one of our T-shirts." Bonnie added that, clearly doing her best to eavesdrop.

I arched an eyebrow.

She shrugged.

"Oh, man. That sucks for you. Wait. Is that good? Because, like, publicity—"

"There *is* such a thing as bad publicity."

"Shit. Like, sorry. Okay, off to call Mum. Later." He cut the line.

I stared at the phone. *Later? When does he think we're going to talk? Come to that, what would we even talk about?*

Malik Fucking Forestal.

I sighed. "Can you do a complete deep dive into Malik Forestal? You seem to know a lot about him."

"Well, Razor Made is Blossom's favorite band."

"Not yours?" Since I hadn't even heard of them, I certainly didn't have a bone in this fight.

"I'm still a classic Grindstone fan. Axel is smoking hot."

Grindstone, I'd heard of. "Aren't they down in the States some-where? And was that the guy...who kissed a guy..." I pressed a hand to my forehead. I was going to need some heavy-duty painkillers very soon. Maybe even my migraine pills.

"Yeah. Axel had a video of him kissing his high school teacher, and he leaked it to the internet. Although if it's a video of you, and you have it, then it's not really leaking, right? It's just uploading—"

"Bonnie."

"Sorry. Yes, Axel uploaded a video of him kissing his teacher—although this was ten years after graduating, and there was nothing going on between them while he was a student—"

"Thank God for that." I didn't know any of these people personally, but I didn't like hearing about shit like that.

"And, yeah, Grindstone is performing at Rocktoberfest again this year. I could tell you all about…" She tapped her phone. "But something tells me you want Malik's history on your desk in an hour."

"Twenty minutes would be better." I offered a weary smile. "But thorough is important."

"I'll send it through in chunks. Take your pills." She plopped into her chair, put on her noise-canceling headphones, cracked her knuckles, and started typing like a madwoman.

Thoroughly exhausted—even though the clock hadn't hit ten—I headed to my office. The layout of this house was traditional—each room separated by doors. Personally, I much preferred the modern approach to having open living spaces, but this setup enabled me to have a private office that I could lock each night after work.

I unlocked my cabinet and pulled out my laptop. I placed it carefully on the desk, then dropped into my chair. After a ten-second debate, I opened my drawer, yanked out my migraine-prevention pills, dry swallowed one, and let out a groan of pain.

Knowing me, I'd left it too long. Tough to balance the moment I realized I was about to get a migraine with the moment it hit and the drugs might no longer be effective.

"Fuck."

Unsatisfying, but necessary.

I pulled my water bottle out of my knapsack and took several long pulls. Lukewarm. Gross. Also didn't have it in me to go to the kitchen to get cold. I'd never ask Bonnie—I wasn't that kind of boss. If she just took upon herself and used her initiative to refill it with cold water, however, I'd thank her profusely. I was great at keeping track of legal precedents and emails from our accountant. Eating and staying hydrated? Not so much.

After letting out another sigh, I opened the laptop and dove into my emails. I started with one from a donor, complaining about seeing our logo splashed across her television screen. She said she wouldn't be contributing anymore. Next came a notice from the bank that our line of credit was getting close to being maxed out.

I checked the calendar—even though I absolutely knew today was the twenty-second. The transfer I'd arranged for the twenty-ninth would cover payroll and most of our bills. And there'd be enough to cover the interest charges on the line of credit. I didn't like carrying that much debt, but the foundation that provided much of our funds paid at bloody inconvenient times, and everything was juggling ten balls in the air and hoping none fell.

My notification pinged.

I winced.

Then, I navigated over to Bonnie's email and opened it.

Jesus.

I nearly swallowed my tongue.

This is Malik Fucking Forestal? Holy crap. Hot. Seriously hot.

His hair struck me first. Black, kinky, and curly.

Next were his lips—plump and completely kissable.

He had high cheekbones, and as I followed his cheeks down to his strong jawline, I considered how I felt about this.

He wore a shirt without sleeves, and his muscles were...impressive.

The tattoos were...stunning. I couldn't make them out with the lighting of the photograph, but I could say I was intrigued.

His chest hair was less than a pelt, but more than a smattering—with tight black curls just waiting to be caressed.

Finally, he wore sunglasses that obscured his eyes. With his dark coloring, I assumed his eyes were dark brown, but I might've been wrong.

I stared at his photograph.

Then noticed the title of the article. *The Next Lenny Kravitz?*

Okay, I didn't know much about music, but I'd heard of Lenny Kravitz. I clicked on the link to his *American Woman* video.

Yikes. Talk about objectification of women. Although that was sort of what the song was about. And the *woman*? I searched and discovered she was actress Heather Graham.

And then I realized I'd spent ten precious minutes going down a rabbit hole that didn't necessarily need going down.

Except...yeah. Malik looked like a young Lenny Kravitz.

So, I clicked on a link to a YouTube video.

And...sat in stunned silence.

Malik playing guitar. Malik singing. Malik making out with...yep, a guy.

Okay, well, that answers an inappropriate question that was swirling in your mind. Yes, he's gay. Or bi. Damn attractive too.

And it'd been a very, very, very long time since I'd gotten laid.

I closed my eyes. Yep, Paul.

Over a year. Not since I'd left the firm. My former coworker

Well, shit. *I need to go down to Davie Street this weekend, find a bar, and damn well find a hookup.* Maybe I'd run into someone I'd turned down in the past because I'd been in a relationship with Paul. I sort of remembered an ironworker with a scar on his face and a bit of an attitude. He'd turned me on—but I'd turned him down. A firefighter? He'd been a ginger and super cute. And I seemed to remember a rugby player...

All these perfectly acceptable men whom I'd turned down because I'd fancied myself in love with my boyfriend.

What a crock of shit that turned out to be.

Another ping had me opening Bonnie's next email.

Vancouver's Favorite Son Moves from Violin to Electric Guitar.

Okay, that had me intrigued as well. I scanned the article that talked about how Malik had been a prodigy on the violin. The accolades he'd received as a young boy. The success as a young man. The tragedy of losing his parents at only twenty-one. Then, finally, his decision to leave the symphony to blaze a trail as a rock star.

The article chronicled his first eighteen months—the struggle to put together a band. Finding rehearsal space. Recording their first album.

I didn't know much about music these days, but I was aware that making music was pretty easy with all the things one could do with a computer. But for quality production, old-fashioned was still best.

More rabbit holes.

What I wasn't seeing was an explanation as to why—

Well, shit.

"I want to do more with my platform. One day I'm going to be a megastar, and if I can elevate causes that are important to me, then that's what I'll do. I have to be strategic, though. Use social media to my advantage."

Okay then, at least I understood a little bit better.

A knock sounded on my door.

"Come in."

Bonnie poked her head around. "Blossom's here. She wants to know when she can release the footage of the arrest."

Never. My gut reaction was a hard *no.* But I didn't control Blossom. I'd make it clear I didn't want the organization anywhere near this shit...but I couldn't actually stop her from releasing it under another user.

I rubbed my forehead and then reached for the painkillers again.

This is going to be a very long day.

Chapter Two

Malik

"Hello, Mama Murthi." I donned my sunglasses as I stepped into the brilliant mid-afternoon sunshine.

Creed's mother—who was all of five-foot-nothing—glared. "You, child, are going to be the death of me. I thought my son was bad. Then he brought you home." She wagged her finger at me. "You're a bad influence on my baby."

I held back the laugh—barely. Her *baby* was five years older than me and had gotten into way more trouble than I ever had. Or even planned to. He would point to his misadventures and would advise me not to travel down that pathway. "I'm sorry, Mama."

At her insistence, I called her that. Her discovery that I was an orphan—if one could be considered an orphan at twenty-five—propelled her into full *mama mode*. Creed's term, not mine. Or it hadn't been. At first. Now I knew how to recognize when her caring nature was pushing through. At the moment? More like legal-aid pit bull.

"I'm sorry."

She put her hands on her hips and glared.

"Really."

"Do you promise to never do it again?"

I put one hand over my heard and held the other out as if I were taking a solemn vow. "I promise to never chain myself to the Lion's Gate Bridge again."

Easy promise to make—that had been part of my condition of release. The cops weren't going to charge me—but they were super annoyed with me. Not that I could blame them. Anytime you caused someone to need bolt cutters wasn't a good day for either of you.

Creed slung an arm over my shoulder. Despite his mother's lack of stature, he was a few inches over me.

I gazed into his dark-brown eyes. "Take me home?"

"Not to your home." Mama shook her fist at me. "You come to my house. I feed you samosas, roti, and French fries."

She pretty much had me at samosas, but French fries sealed the deal. "My favorites?"

"I bought a bag just for you the other day. I told Creed that you'd need them sooner or later."

Creed, who still lived at home, grinned. "She bought me pierogies."

Mama rolled her eyes. "I try to raise you right, and your go-to comfort food is Ukrainian?"

"Uh, I think pierogies are Polish." I squinted as I gazed around to see if any members of the press or fans might be around. I'd asked to be allowed a quick detour to the bathroom. Ostensibly to piss, but I'd ensured my hair was perfect, and I wasn't too sweaty. I should've been frozen, given the Arctic temperatures in that building. Except that cop had me believing her partner was preparing charging documents for the Crown Prosecutor as we sat here.

More fool me. He'd been doing a Starbucks run. He'd even brought me a black coffee and had warned me not to pull another stunt like that because no way was the Vancouver Police Department going to let me go second time. Then he'd advised me an angry Indian woman was waiting for me and I better show some contrition because he knew Ms. Murthi, and she was not to be trifled with.

Aside from the exceedingly rapid trip to the restroom, I'd hustled.

To find Mama just as pissed as the officer had promised.

"Creed drove us so he'll take us home." She eyed me. "You have everything?"

I held up my coat. "I traveled light."

She narrowed her eyes. "You planned on getting arrested."

I shrugged.

Creed snickered.

Mama shook her finger. "You want to go do that thing down in—" She snapped her fingers.

"Black Rock." Creed was quicker than me to supply that. "Rock-toberfest."

"Right." She rolled her *r*. "Well, if you get arrested, you can't go to—" She flailed her hand.

"Nevada. United States." Creed's glare directed at me matched his mama's.

Oops.

A consequence that hadn't occurred to me while I'd been busy chaining myself to the rail of the bridge. "Well…" Nope. Couldn't come up with a single good excuse. I would've been fucked if they'd charged me. And that had never occurred to me.

"You used to be such a nice boy—before you hooked up with my Creed."

I'd never actually *hooked up* with her son. We'd sized each other up, confirmed we were both tops, and had become friends instead. That was nearly two years ago—just after I left the orchestra. As I was beginning my rebirth.

"I want to say your parents would be disappointed except I didn't know them—God rest their souls—and that would be a cruel thing to say."

And yet she'd thought it...which showed the depth of her disappointment.

"I'll do better. I promise." How hard could it possibly be? Just because the higher ups at TLIO were sticks-in-the-mud, didn't mean I couldn't be inventive. "Hey, is that a news camera?" I pointed toward a van with a television logo on it.

Creed snagged my arm and forcefully pushed me in the opposite direction.

"Hey!"

"You want roti and French fries?"

"Yeah—"

"Then walk quickly to the car, get in the back seat, and for God's sake, keep your mouth shut. She was having a bad day *before* you got brought into the police station. It hasn't exactly been looking up since."

"Oh, I didn't know." I kept walking.

"You didn't have any way of knowing." He sighed. "You can be self-centered, Malik. You know I'm saying this because I love you, right? Just...maybe think about other people now and again?"

I hated when someone couched something harsh with *because I love you*.

Creed *did* love me. We were as tight as brothers.

Mama *did* love me. She wouldn't take the time to try to improve me if she didn't.

But those loves just weren't enough. I'd been an only child—completely doted on by my parents. That gaping hole—that gaping wound—just was never going to be healed. No matter how many people claimed to *love me*, and there were many, it didn't satisfy the needy child who felt abandoned in the world.

Or so my therapist told me when I'd spoken to her about this.

Mama had insisted I go when I was having a rough time last winter.

The psychologist offered some insights and gave me things to try—but she hadn't been able to fix what was really broken inside me.

I allowed Creed to shove me into the back seat of his Nissan Sentra—which was way too fricking small—while his mother settled herself in the front.

He hotfooted around to the driver's seat, and we pulled out of the parking spot and into traffic with absolute ease.

Disgruntled, I snorted. I was never able to navigate traffic the way my friend was. Whichever way I chose—that was the slowest route. If I tried to squeeze in as the last car on an advanced green, I wound up blocking the intersection and making everybody mad at me.

Which I didn't want to do.

I was sensitive that way.

If I drove up Granville Street, I was guaranteed to catch every red light.

Creed could make the same drive and hit every green.

I tried to see if our speeds were different, but I couldn't tell. He was bold, yet cautious. I was forceful, yet disastrous. Somehow, I'd only gotten into two fender-benders. Neither my fault. I stopped. The guys behind me didn't. They hit me. More frustrations dealing with the insurance company and repair shops.

"Smile, Malik. You avoided a clusterfuck. Hey!" Creed exclaimed the word after his mother whacked him on the shoulder. "I'm just being honest."

"Don't use that language around your mother." She met my gaze in the rearview mirror.

I noted she didn't say not to use that language *at all*. She knew her son.

She knew me.

Twenty minutes later, Creed parked his car in front of his family's home in the Champlain Heights district in Killarney—the most southeastern part of Vancouver. During rush hour, the drive was almost twice as long because this was as far from the cop shop as pretty much any two places could be in the city.

Mama Murthi was the first out, and she hustled up the walkway.

I was slower to get out of the car. "You need a bigger ride."

Creed grinned. "I'm just fine—in the driver's seat. Your ride still at your house?"

"Yep. Figured it would be safest there." At the house I inherited upon my parents' death in the tonier and more affluent Arbutus Ridge. More house than a single man needed, but I couldn't bear to part with my legacy. Plus, one of the very few owned by a Black family in that neighborhood—something I never forgot.

"You know she's going to make you pay for this clusterfuck."

I rolled my eyes. He was right. Of everyone in the world, his mother most had the ability to make me pay for things. Because disappointing Mama wasn't just hard on my heart, it was bad for my health. I only ate junk food at home. Here, in the Murthi household, I got fresh fruits, vegetables, and other healthy fare. "She's not really that pissed, is she?"

He snickered. "She's feeding you...so I'd say you'll eventually be forgiven." He sobered. "She's right about the States. You want to follow in Grindstone's footsteps, right?"

"At least two years at Rocktoberfest? You bet."

"Well, getting arrested will bar you from visiting the States. No Nevada. No Black Rock. No Rocktoberfest." He slammed his car door. "Look, I get where you're coming from. The pipelines across tribal lands are—"

"Immoral? Inhumane? Cruel?"

He closed one eye—a guarantee he was deep in thought. "I was going to say *wrong* but sure, let's place even more significance on the actions than they deserve."

"More?" I sputtered. "Pristine wilderness destroyed. Water polluted forever. Animals forced from their homes. Treaties violated." I stopped to take a breath.

My friend merely stood there.

"I get it. They aren't even my lands. These aren't my disputes. I'm just some city-dwelling guy who doesn't have a bone in this fight."

"All that is very true. But you're allowed to be passionate—just not at the risk of getting arrested. What will you do if you can't tour in the States? How will we get a good record deal?"

"Lots of bands are avoiding the States these days. Traveling is just dangerous."

He pursed his lips. "Sixty percent of our sales come from the US. Sure, we've got a big following in Canada. As well as in Europe—Latvia in particular. Can you explain that to me?"

As he well knew, I could not explain why Latvians loved our sound so much. Who could explain anything these days? Things felt perpetually out of kilter. Like nothing made sense. Much of that had to do with losing my parents. A lot of it, though, had to do with geopolitical unrest around the world. The experts might claim we were living in the most peaceful time in all of human history—but it sure didn't feel like it. "Samosas?"

Creed rolled his eyes. "You bet. I'll even make that yogurt dessert you like so much."

Which took very little effort, but I wasn't going to point that out to him. He was a good friend, and I appreciated that.

Mama stood on the threshold to the house. "That cute reporter guy is interviewing another cute guy, and I think you'll want to see this."

I blinked. "Huh?"

"That Indian dude she adores. Probably. That would be the *cute reporter guy.*"

We headed toward the house.

"No clue about the other *cute guy.* You know Mama—she's always wanting to set you up with a nice respectable man."

"Isn't the reporter married?"

"And more than twice your age? Yes. So I'm thinking the other guy is the reason she's hustling us."

Since one didn't keep Mama waiting, we hustled into the house and straight into the living room with the large-screen television. Much larger than Mama would've chosen—but perfect for Papa whose vision wasn't so good these days. For watching cricket, football, and darts—lawn, though, not the kind at bars.

The Indian reporter, with his tan-colored skin and threads of silver at his temples stood and spoke to—

"Son of a bitch."

"Malik." Mama glared.

"What? That's Spencer Wainright. He's the figurehead of This Land is Ours. But he never does anything. Why are they interviewing him? They should be interviewing me." I nearly stomped my foot.

Wanting to be invited back in the future kept that impulse in check.

"Why do you think chaining oneself to the railing of the Lion's Gate Bridge is an ineffective tool of protest?" Gorgeous Indian silver fox asked the question.

"Our organization believes in grass-roots movements—and we did hold up traffic for a few minutes this morning to get our point across. But inconveniencing a few commuters for a few minutes is very different from causing traffic chaos for an extended period of time. That we don't approve of."

"So Malik Forestal isn't part of your organization?"

"We have many members who join us. Who attend our rallies and demonstrations. We did not approve, nor do we condone, what Mr. Forestal did today. He was looking for social media likes and clicks. Our organization's goals are much deeper than that. More...substantive."

I saw red.

Chapter Three

B lossom glared.

"What?" I met that glare with a confused look of my own. I couldn't fathom why she was pissed with me. "I thought the interview went well." The reporter had been fair, competent, and someone I'd dealt with before. Kind of cute. And married—happily, as far as I knew—with children and, apparently, a grandchild. He was yummy, in a silver fox kind of way, but I hadn't been looking at him that way.

Much.

Nope.

I'd been obsessing over a certain too-handsome-for-his-own-good rock star who'd given me a migraine yesterday, even though we'd yet to meet in person.

Blossom crossed her arms across her abundant bosom. I didn't normally notice these things—or tried not to—but she always wore clothes that emphasized her...ample cleavage. She also had long, flowing blonde hair that was always tousled in *that* way and big, beguiling, blue eyes.

When she recruited volunteers, we had scores of guys, and quite a few gals, lining up to follow her as if she were the pied piper.

She sighed. "You should've consulted me."

"Blossom, you handle *social* media. Don't get me wrong, you do a fantastic job."

"*Media*, Spencer. You needed a media-relations person guiding you. Coaching you. Stopping you from making stupid mistakes."

"Hey, I didn't make any stupid mistakes." *Did I?* "I was fine."

"You weren't fine. You didn't even cope."

"I did okay. I have some savvy, you know."

"And how did your legal background prepare you for dealing with the media? Please give me the precise educational background—or work experience—that made you vaguely qualified to go up against a professional like him?"

We both knew who *he* was.

"I worked in the biomedical research field for years. They put out plenty of press releases and held media events."

Blossom's eyebrow arched. "Right. And how many of those press releases did you write? How many media events did you host?"

"Well—"

"Hell, Spencer. Did you even attend these vaunted *events*?"

I held in the wince.

Barely.

You're the boss. "I did what I thought was best."

Blossom slashed the air. "Razor Made is an up-and-coming band with a small, but very loyal fanbase. You pissed some of them off last night. They could make it difficult to recruit people to our cause in the future."

Oh God, what if she has a point? I'd been focused on clearing the organization's name—not about future recruitments. In fact, I'd convinced myself the inverse was true—if people thought we were only doing law-abiding work, then they'd be more likely to join. We didn't want troublemakers. Guys like—

"I want to see him." A firm voice came from the reception area. A very strong, masculine voice.

"He's in a meeting right now." Bonnie—just as strong and clear.

"Oh my God. He's here." Blossom squealed and then fanned herself.

Yep, fanned herself.

As much as I didn't want to admit to knowing who *he* was, clearly the cause of all yesterday's distress had shown up.

"You can't go in there—" Bonnie, again putting up a good front. Except she was about five-five and a little on the slender side. To the best of my knowledge, she didn't have martial arts training—and I didn't want her engaging in physical combat for my sake anyway.

"It's okay, Bonnie. You can let Mr. Forestal in."

Blossom grinned.

My office door was thrust open, and *he* stepped into my inner sanctuary.

That invasion raised my hackles right away. I didn't want anyone in here whom I hadn't specifically invited. I needed this to be my place of peace. I even had a vanilla-scented candle and soft music playing in the background. If incense didn't give me a headache, I'd burn that as well. I might be a logical lawyer, but I also believed in encouraging good juju.

The influence of my beatnik parents who were born a dozen years too late. They wanted to be hippies protesting war. Instead, they'd embraced the *no nukes* movement with great fervor.

But none of that calm helped now.

Malik stood before me.

He was a couple of inches shorter, but from the distance, our eyes met.

Ha, I was right. Dark brown. Stunning and luminous dark-brown eyes. His black hair curled wildly and I wondered about the texture.

Today he wore loose khaki shorts that exposed his knees and calves. That shouldn't have been sexy—but it was. He wore a loose cotton shirt, with several buttons undone.

"Aren't you cold?"

Right because that *is the most important thing going on at the moment.*

I wore jeans, a henley, and a cardigan.

Early October had been a slow end to summer, weather-wise. Around Thanksgiving, the weather had turned cold and wet. Yesterday might've had brilliant sunshine, but the temperature had hovered around sixty. Today, so far, it was even lower.

He blinked. "Excuse me?"

"You're wearing sandals and shorts. The temperature is too low for such clothes."

"Who do you think you are, my mother?"

The response of *a good mother wouldn't let her son go out in inappropriate clothes* was on the tip of my tongue. Before I could spit it out, though, I remembered his mother had died tragically. That, unless he had other relatives, he was lacked parental figures. "I just meant you should dress appropriately."

He gave me a long perusal.

Long.

Slow.

Examination.

Don't fidget. You still have the high ground. You were right. He was wrong.

Still, heat rose to my cheeks as his gaze met mine. I wanted to ask what he saw, but the dismissive flicker in his eyes assured me he wasn't having positive thoughts about me. "Can I help you? I have work to do—"

"You're an asshole."

Blossom, blessed woman, giggled.

I glared.

She held up her phone.

Is she asking if she can record this? Is she suggesting she should leave and will make more social media posts? And while we're asking inane questions...who exactly is the boss? "Can I help you?"

"My phone is blowing up with notifications." She pointed her phone toward Malik.

He offered a shy smile. Which morphed into amused. Which changed into predatory.

His ability to pivot so quickly—three solidly different looks in less than thirty seconds—took my breath away. Or perhaps that was because he turned that wolfish grin on me.

Our gazes clashed...then held.

Blossom slipped from the room and closed the door once she was in the reception area.

Since I still stood behind my desk, I gestured for him to sit on one of the two chairs facing me. *At least I wasn't sitting down—at least I still have some dignity.* I needed to repeat this since my cock was becoming very interested in whatever Malik thought he was offering.

Maybe he's not offering anything at all. Maybe this is all in your imagination. Although Malik made no attempt to hide his gay liaisons—I'd spent way too much time with my search engine last night—I didn't share quite so freely. My staff knew I was gay. None of us, though, shared that information far and wide. That fact wasn't necessary for anyone who dealt with me to know. They should see me as the competent leader of this organization—not a queer man who lived in Vancouver. *Enough navel gazing.* "How can I help you?"

Malik cocked his head. "Are you going to act like nothing happened?"

I put my hand on my hip—clearly we weren't sitting. "What happened? You got taken away by the police yesterday after chaining yourself to a bridge. That wasn't behavior this organization condones. Blocking traffic for a few minutes is one thing. Forcing police officers to put themselves at risk—"

"No one was at risk—"

"Nice try, Mr. Forestal. I saw the footage. Those two officers did have to imperil themselves to get you unchained. Things could have gone badly—for all three of you. This isn't something we could ever support. I was just making that clear."

"By going to CNC? The Canadian News Channel? That's the only interview I caught. Were there more? You went to their studio—and met with the important anchor. That meant your *discussion* wasn't an impromptu thing."

So much to unpack in those words. I tried to sort out where his anger was coming from—but I couldn't put my finger on it. "Was it the choice of network, that anchor in particular, or the fact I made arrangements that bothers you the most?"

He glared. "Perhaps the words you said?"

"Oh." I wracked my brains. I'd said a lot of things, but when I'd watched the interview later, it'd been edited. *Was something out of context? Everything seemed pretty clear to me.*

"Which words?"

"Likes and clicks."

"Ah." His retort brought things into sharp focus. "Well, if you don't like being referred to as a want-to-be-celebrity, perhaps you shouldn't act like one. Now, I have work to—"

"Where do you get off?" He spat out the words. "You don't know me. You don't know anything about me."

"Well, considering much of your life is splashed across—"

"You checked me out?" In a heartbeat, his anger morphed back into predatory.

I rolled my eyes. "Of course I checked you out. You're claiming to represent this organization. This group means everything to me—"

"You mean it pays your bills."

"What?" I frowned.

"You draw a salary."

I pressed a hand to my temple. *Fuck, not now. Not fucking now.* But migraines would wait for no one, and stress was a huge trigger. *So why did you take this job?* "Yes, I am paid. This is my full-time employment. I don't have enough money to live if I don't pay myself. I'm paid at parity with many others and less than still more. I'm making far less in this job than I did in my last—"

"Why'd you leave?"

"What?" I fought not to squint.

"Your last job? Why did you leave such a lucrative position to take a cut in salary and a job you're not even good at?"

"Hey, that's rude. You don't know me. You don't know what I do around here. You waltz in with your attitude and your ignorance—"

"I am not ignorant." He said the words with low menace. "And you haven't answered my question."

Because I'm not going to. You don't deserve to know something so personal. So intimate. That's between me, Pike, and his God. I didn't have a God. I might've before my friend's death, but I certainly didn't have one now. If pressed, I might've said Mother Nature. That was about as good as it got. "I'm not answering your question, Mr. Forestal. You can see yourself out and please do not do anything illegal in our name again. The members of This Land is Ours will not be thanking you. We don't need unwarranted scrutiny. We just want to—"

"What are you hiding?"

Geometric patterns danced in the periphery of my vision. *Fuck, fuck, fuckety fuck.* From this moment on, nothing good was going to happen. "I need you to leave."

"I'm not finished. We're going to hash this out, you're going to apologize—"

"Fine. I'm sorry. I was wrong. You're a good guy. Now please get out of my office." *You just need to hold it together for a little bit longer. You'll be okay if—*

"What's wrong?"

His face swam as tears filled my eyes. Even through the physiological reactions my body was enduring, I could spot the concern. "Just go." My voice broke. My knees wobbled as indescribable pain crashed through my temples. A screwdriver into my brain.

"Yeah. Okay." He turned and stalked out.

I dropped heavily into my chair. I opened my drawer, but I couldn't sort out which pill bottle I needed.

"I've got it. The strong ones?" Bonnie was there, placing each bottle on the desk and scanning the labels.

"Yeah."

"Right." She opened the bottle, dropped two pills on my hand, and pressed my water bottle into the other.

I downed the pills.

Then I let her guide me to my couch. I let her put an icepack on my forehead. I let her close the blinds, turn off the music, and quietly close the door as she let herself out.

I didn't remember anything beyond that.

Chapter Four

Malik

"What is his problem?" I sipped my coffee in the Starbucks on Hastings Street.

Blossom sat across from me and, even as I stared at her, her gaze didn't waver from her phone. She did, however, stop her rapid-fire typing for a moment. "Bonnie won't say, but he's got some kind of medical condition. I worry about his blood pressure sometimes, you know? He goes kind of purple. And he's like, old." She resumed her furious thumb tapping.

I might've been of the instant-messaging generation, but my thumbs were too big and clumsy on the keyboard. I relied on predictive word choice and sheer determination to create my messages.

Oh, and I kept them bloody short.

"He's not *that* old." The guy had overlong blond hair that kind of framed his face. He had powerful green eyes—sort of moss-colored. He was just a couple inches taller than me—about Creed's height. But where my friend was slender, this guy was more muscular. Hard to tell his measurements under that grandfather cardigan. *Seriously, a cardigan? Who the fuck wears those?* I snuck a peek out the window at the darkening skies.

Mama Murthi had said something about a rainstorm this afternoon and had wagged her finger at my sandals and shorts. But hey, weather like this deserved to be honored with shorts and T-shirts. We hadn't hit winter yet, for crying out loud. I'd be digging out my winter coat soon enough—why welcome the season with open arms when I could cling to summer just a little bit longer?

"Malik?"

"Hmm?" I turned my attention back to Blossom, who had ceased typing. The woman was a force of nature, and her pouty lips pursed. "We're getting tons of traction. Especially with the picture I posted of you just now."

"Uh, which picture?"

She turned her phone, and I gazed. "Oh, that one." The one where I faced the camera and was grinning—while thinking about stripping Spencer naked and fucking him over his desk. I didn't *know* he was gay...but his close examination of me—instead of the outright dismissal I'd expected—had me perking up in all kinds of ways. And thinking all kinds of lascivious thoughts. "That's a good shot."

"Too bad I couldn't get one with you and Spencer. Man, that would be..." She wrinkled her nose.

I waited with bated breath.

"Hot. I mean, you two are super-hot. And to have both of you together? An eleven on the sex meter."

"Oh, is Spencer gay?"

She snorted. Then sobered. "Oh, right. Uh...yes. But maybe don't tell anyone? He's more interested in being known as a social justice warrior than as a gay man. Personally, I think that's all bullshit. We are who we are. We love who we love. I can say, I love everyone."

Ah, my unabashed pansexual friend. Well, we were friendly. That counted.

Right?

I saluted her with my ceramic mug and took another sip. "Totally agree."

"We need a photo with the two of you. Maybe looking over some documents? He looks totally sexy in his reading glasses. The glasses he doesn't want anyone to know he wears."

Picturing Spencer in black-framed glasses perched on his nose was easy. He'd look up from his desk, over the rims, and give me a *come fuck me* look. I'd crawl under his desk and give him a blow job while he—

"Malik." Blossom waved her hand in front of my face.

"Hmm?"

"Sheesh, you're as distractible as he is." She chewed her fingernail. "In fact, we were discussing you when he got this sort of weird look on his face. I had to snap his attention to me as well."

"I'm paying attention."

"Are you? Really? Because I'm not getting that sense at all. Your head's in the clouds. Are you thinking about Grindstone? They're performing tonight, right?"

"Yep. I know a guy who's going to try to record their new song on his phone. I mean, the recording will be crap, but I'm supercurious. They haven't performed in a while, and I'm wondering what Axel's been up to."

Blossom pursed her lips.

Uh-oh. "But we're focused on today."

"When's Razor Made's next concert?"

"We don't have anything for a couple of weeks. We've got several practices lined up and one day in the recording studio. We know which track we want to lay down, and we've got one day to do it."

"Have you thought any more about writing a theme for This Land is Ours?"

Oops. "I keep meaning to. Just...that feels inadequate, you know? For the magnitude of the problems we're facing. The existentialism and all that."

"Exactly." She tapped her perfectly manicured nail on the table.

"When's the next protest?"

"There's something in late November."

"That far out?"

"Well, the Vancouver city council is meeting about a bylaw amendment. It's not directly linked to a pipeline, but it's definitely a step backward in the climate change fight. I think Spencer's secured a spot to speak. He'll be busy preparing for that."

"When's the meeting?"

"Monday night."

A plan started to coalesce in my mind. I had some research to do this weekend—along with jamming. Yeah, I could juggle both. I snagged my phone and sent a message to our band's group chat, reminding everyone we were gathering in my basement this weekend. My parents had created a rehearsal space for me—for my violin—but I'd spent some money after they died, converting it into a bigger space.

The house was far away from both our neighbors, so sound wasn't an issue. Acoustics was, though, and my basement setup was the best of all the places we could hang—except the actual recording studio, of course.

Creed, Reese, and Freddie all sent thumbs-ups.

Blossom tried to see my screen.

"Just the guys acknowledging we're meeting at my place this week-end."

"Reese, too?"

I frowned. "Well, yeah."

"Reese identifies as female, right?"

"Yeah." *Where is she going with this? Is she interested in Reese?*

"Well, if Reese identifies as female, then maybe *guys* isn't the right term. Maybe say *folks*?"

I wrinkled my nose. "Mama and Papa Murthi are Creed's *folks*. That term doesn't suit my bandmates." Although her point about inclusivity was noted.

She shrugged. "I just don't want Reese to feel excluded."

I snickered. "Reese is practically in charge of all of us. Bassist extra-ordinaire. Talented musician. Fantastic composer. Her lyrics usually need polishing—that's what I'm for."

"You fix Reese's lyrics?"

"I...yeah, fix them. There really isn't another word. She tells me what she's trying to say, and I...make it happen."

"A team."

"Yeah."

"So call them your *teammates*. Or *bandmates*. Just pick something gender neutral."

Knowing Blossom was right, and actually acknowledging that out loud, were two very different things. "I'll try to do better."

"Do. There is no try. Crap."

I frowned, then followed her gaze outside.

Crap indeed.

The rain poured down in sheets. "How'd that happen?"

She chuckled. "You need me to explain the anatomy of a rainstorm? I think it has something to do with nimbocumulous—"

"That's not a thing."

"Sure it is. They're a type of cloud—

"There's cumulous and nimbostratus—"

"Seriously? You actually paid attention in science class?"

Now's probably not the time to explain about parents who wanted a prodigal child in all possible subjects—not just classical music and violin. "I, uh, found cloud class interesting."

"Cloud class? Is that a thing?"

I waved her off. "Neither here nor there."

"If you say so. Since you paid so much attention, maybe you could have predicted the rain?"

"My friend's mother's knees predicted the rain. The meteorologist predicted the rain. I just figured I had time, you know?"

"Well, can you give me a ride so I don't look like a waterlogged rat when I arrive home? I have a date tonight."

I wasn't certain what getting wet at one in the afternoon had to do with a *date tonight*, but I figured it had something to do with hair. For me, everything was about my hair. "Yeah, I can drive you. Smart not to own a car in this city."

"And yet you do."

I shrugged. My parents crashed in my dad's car. Right into an abutment. They never stood a chance. I inherited my mother's electric SUV. At least I didn't have to feel as guilty as if I were using a gas guzzler. Vancouver's electricity was pulled from a hydro dam up north—so, clean energy. "I'm going to get a refill on my coffee, grab a sandwich, and then we can head out."

"Sure...oh, I gotta watch this video."

I left her to it and sauntered up to the counter. I ordered a venti black coffee, a breakfast sandwich—even though we were clearly into the afternoon—and waited patiently while the barista toasted the food.

Blossom laughed. She had one of those infectious laughs—the kind that everyone found easy to follow because it just tinkled. When I heard it, I always smiled.

Yesterday had been the first time I'd come out to an actual TLIO event, even though I'd been communicating regularly with Blossom and talking up the group—and the mission—to everyone. I couldn't explain why I'd felt compelled yesterday, or why I'd brought along a chain, but I didn't have any regrets.

If they'd charged you, and you couldn't go to Black Rock next year, then you would've had bucket loads of regrets. Creed, Reese, and Freddie would've killed you.

Okay.

Maybe.

Probably.

The barista handed me my sandwich in a little paper bag. "There you go," He batted his eyelashes.

I smiled. "Thanks for this." I caught his grin turning into a pout just as I pivoted to head toward the door where Blossom waited.

"Grindstone's performing tonight, right?"

"Uh, yeah." I eyed the rain. "Does it look like it might ease up?"

"Nope. We're just going to have to run for it."

"Our hair is going to get wet."

She cocked her head. "Yeah, sorry about that. Not that I can control the weather or anything. I mean, we could just try to wait it out—"

"Heavy all day." The barista, who was wiping the coffee stand, offered us a sheepish smile.

I wasn't entirely thrilled he'd been eavesdropping, but this was a coffeeshop—so discretion and privacy weren't exactly guaranteed.

"I don't suppose you have a spare umbrella." Blossom gave him her most-charming smile.

You bat for the wrong team, dear. Not that they guy couldn't do it out of the goodness of his heart.

He shook his head. "Sorry. My mom drops me off and picks me up."

I blinked. The guy had to be about my age. At least I was driving myself around by the time I was nineteen. Admittedly in her car, but at least I'd been independent and mobile.

"Well, thanks." Blossom turned to me. "We run?"

I clicked the remote to unlock the door. "We run."

And we did.

Both completely soaked by the time we shut the car doors.

She giggled. "Okay, that was refreshing."

"Just be glad we didn't have any paperwork." I flipped on the defogger to clear the windshield. "You don't want to come over?"

"Date."

I pointed to the clock. "In, like, five hours."

She grabbed a lock of her straggly wet hair.

I sighed, started the car, and pulled out of the spot. The windshields were clear, so I was able to drive without a problem. I kept my speed on the low side, though, because the sheets of rain made visibility tough. "Good thing we were out yesterday and not today. What happened to all that sun?"

"Storm coming in off the Pacific. That happens in the autumn, you know."

"And it's only going to get worse. We're in for another dreary winter." I stopped at a red light.

"Yeah?" She pulled a compact out of her huge purse and started fluffing her hair. "How do you know this stuff?"

"How do you not know this stuff?" I gestured to her phone with my elbow. "You're always on that thing. You don't check weather and news?"

"Uh...I have notifications and stuff for certain things—weather isn't one of them. Oh, but the Canucks won last night."

The light turned green, and I advanced into the intersection—after looking both ways. "Yeah? Do you know the amount of greenhouse gases a Zamboni emits?"

"Nope, but I'm certain you can tell me. I'm a left up ahead."

We'd discussed where we lived at some point, and she'd said near Victoria Drive and First Avenue.

Completely in the opposite direction from my house, but I didn't care. *Not like I have anywhere else to be.*

When she'd asked about me, I'd vaguely pointed west and said *that way*. In truth, Arbutus Ridge was one of the more expensive neighborhoods in Vancouver—and that was saying something. People made certain assumptions when they heard where I lived. So I just didn't tell them. Seemed easier that way.

"Right here, and I'm the third house."

I followed her directions and pulled up before a stately turn-of-the-last-century home. Painted funky purple with light-green accents. *Oh, okay. Boho chic?* "This looks nice."

"It's a room I can afford. There are ten of us, but I get my own bedroom, so that's nice. Better than Chilliwack."

I cocked my head.

"Oh, Cedar Valley's nice and all, but getting from the Wack into Vancouver's pretty brutal if you don't have a car. And my parents were never willing to lend me theirs. I came here for college—media studies—and I just kind of stayed."

"But you graduated." She'd mentioned that in one of our conversations.

"Yeah, but getting a paid job is tough these days. In my field of study, anyway. I make way more as an influencer."

I understood the words she spoke, but their meaning escaped me. I didn't understand how influencers made money at all. Product endorsements paid *that* much?

"Well, it's nice of you to help with TLIO."

My wipers were running at full speed, and I could barely see the house. *This is nuts.*

"Looks good on my résumé. I'm going to land a paying job at a nonprofit or something one of these days. I even have plans to get my own apartment."

Good luck with that. Rents were insane in this city. Buying was even crazier—although not by much. I knew how lucky I was...but still resented having everything handed to me at the same time. I'd give it all back to have my parents still alive. "Well, have fun tonight."

"I will. Let me know if you get footage of the concert." She pecked my cheek and was gone before I could respond.

Once she was inside the house, I double-checked behind me, and pulled into traffic.

And drove slowly home.

Chapter Five

Spencer

"What are you staring at?" Through one slitted eye, I faced my demon.

Well, my rescue cat Moses.

Who, for the record, I hadn't named.

I always felt obliged to explain that to people. Not just because I didn't want them to think I was religious—because I wasn't. But also because I didn't want folks thinking he was more special than he was.

Indolently, he licked his paw.

He's a legend in his own mind.

I scratched behind his ear.

He nuzzled against my hand and started to purr.

The sound vibrated down my arm and into my chest—or so it felt. Calm enveloped me—or that's what I told myself.

Moses had been discovered next to his dead mother and three siblings in an abandoned lot. No way should he have made it. Hence the rescue agency naming him Moses and nursing him back to health.

I'd read about the biblical Moses and couldn't find the thread between that and this guy's impossible odds survival, but whatever. He was ten weeks old when he was finally healthy enough to be adopted.

Happenstance.

Pike's memorial service had been on a Thursday and I went into the animal-rescue shelter on a Friday, and Moses had come home with me on a Saturday. From death to resurrection in three days.

Because I had no doubt Pike lived and breathed in this demon cat I'd rescued.

I'd been led to believe he was quiet, unassuming, and loved snuggles.

Right.

Nope.

He was destructive, mouthy, and had massive attitude.

Also, with him being my first cat, I couldn't tell if I'd been hoodwinked by the rescue shelter or if he'd hoodwinked them. Somehow, this demonic force wasn't the bill of goods I'd been sold.

And yet I'd never considered returning him.

Even when he peed on my favorite shoes the morning of an important conference.

He'd been neutered, of course. But that didn't stop him from randomly peeing on things—usually when he felt neglected. Which meant I spent an inordinate amount of time trying to ensure he didn't feel neglected.

I'd even watched videos of this woman who had trained her cat to talk.

Well, the cat had fifty buttons to push expressing different things—from objects to emotions and everything in between. The lady's cat *spoke* to her. No question. I watched those videos, and I saw a cat who understood how to express her needs.

My cat liked to chase laser pointers and dig up potted plants.

The ten buttons I'd bought for him to attempt communication with me were mothballed in my closet.

"You want food?"

He just blinked at me. As if saying, *duh. I always want food. What a stupid question.* No matter how much I fed him, he never put on weight. He was still scrappy and scrawny. The vet assured me that he was perfectly healthy and I didn't need to worry. I trusted her. I also wanted a substantive cat who didn't look like a breath of wind might knock him over. When guests came to visit, I always found myself explaining about his history—lest people think I was starving him.

I gazed at the clock radio.

Six-thirty.

I tested my head.

Not great.

Not bad.

Just...not great.

I closed my eyes for a moment.

Wait...six-thirty in the morning or evening?

I replayed what I could remember.

Malik.

And...?

Bonnie shoving me into a cab during a rainstorm and telling me to hunker down until the storm passed.

I checked my bladder.

Yeah, I had to piss.

Still not having a clue whether I was still living through Friday or if we'd tipped over into Saturday morning, I rolled out of bed and staggered to the bathroom.

Never so grateful to have the nightlight, I pissed and tried to orient myself. This time of year, six-thirty meant dark. The blackout drapes in my bedroom ensured no crack of light came into the space. I had the clock radio on dim, a nightlight in that room, and a nightlight in here.

I flushed the toilet, washed my hands, and then splashed cold water on my face.

Nope, still clueless.

Because you took the heavy-duty drugs.

I cursed. Several great new migraine prevention drugs had come onto the market in recent years—and I was allergic to one of the ingredients. A bad reaction after trying the med had landed me in the hospital, and all my hopes of relief had been dashed.

Fucking migraines.

I'd had them since childhood. Had memories of my parents dragging me to protests while suffering from them. Being handed a pill, a bottle of water, and a pair of sunglasses.

My parents who cared so much about the planet and the fate of civilization kind of didn't really care about their own child.

That's not fair. They were obsessed with...the bigger picture.

Well, I was never going to be like that.

What, and neglect your cat? It's not like you're ever going to have a kid to neglect.

Sometimes I hated the fucking voice in my head.

If I were a woman, it would be haranguing me about my *biological clock.*

Ship's sailed. I'm on the other side of forty now.

Not that people in their forties couldn't have children. They most certainly could.

I just wasn't going to be one of them. I'd had my chance to prioritize family over career—and I hadn't taken it. Nope. I'd chosen my job. I'd believed I was fighting for the greater good.

Jesus, how fucking naïve were you?

Good question.

A *corporate* lawyer working for a *corporation*.

I'd understood about profit margins. About the almighty dollar. I'd believed the company I worked for was different.

Again, Jesus, how fucking naïve were you?

Well, at least I'd walked away when I found them falsifying research to obtain further government funding.

After turning them in, of course.

Which begged the question how fucking naïve they'd been—thinking I wasn't going to do the right thing. That I'd just turn a blind eye to fraud.

Ha, more fool them.

My phone buzzed.

Okay, six-thirty in the evening.

Probably.

I made my way over to my nightstand as the phone buzzed again. I held the thing at a distance where I could read it. *Should've grabbed my reading glasses. Oh well.* Then the name on the call display registered.

Mom.

Fuck.

I swiped to accept the call as I dropped onto the side of the bed. "Hello, Mother."

"Hello, Spencer. We need to talk."

I tried to suppress the yawn. Yep, in the evening. I'd only had a couple hours' rest. "About what?"

"About your appearance on CNC last night."

More confirmation. This time, I let the yawn happen. Man, I was going to sleep tonight.

"Am I boring you?"

"Of course not, Mother. Just...I had a bad migraine earlier today, and I'm still recovering and—"

"Did you try those essential oils my naturopath recommended?"

I rolled my eyes. I was all for alternative medicines, and I held naturopaths in great respect.

The exception being my mother's. That guy was just a quack. With several complaints lodged against him. To Mother, that was a badge of honor—that the establishment was pushing him to conform and he was resisting the order to change his ways.

I saw the well-founded complaints as a sign that the guy really shouldn't be practicing medicine. Of any kind. "I didn't get an opportunity."

She clucked her tongue. "Spencer, if these things are as bad as you claim, you really should be trying his remedies. They work—"

"*If* they are as bad as I claim?" I held in the annoyance—but barely. "Mother, they're debilitating. And since that's not why you called, why don't you get to the point so I can move on with my life?"

"Is that any way to speak to your mother?"

I thought I'd been quite polite. Given how angry she was making me. "Yes, Mother."

"You were very harsh and rude to Malik."

I pressed a hand to my forehead. "I spoke the truth, Mother. You taught me to always be honest."

"That boy was making a point. He was willing to risk himself. When have you ever done anything so daring? When your father and I were protesting Reagan..."

This, too, shall pass. She'll eventually wear herself out. You just have to—

"Are you listening?"

"Yes, Mother. Ballistic missiles and submarines."

Which made me think of Sean Connery in *The Hunt for Red October.*

Yummy.

"I'm just saying that Malik's heart is in the right place."

"If you say so." I flashed to the angry man in my office this morning. *Was it really just this morning?* And how my body had reacted in a way I hadn't expected. I'd known the man was attractive. I just hadn't predicted how the up-close and personal would actually feel. Then, of course, my body betrayed me and I got the migraine.

"I do say so. You should use him more often. He should be your front man."

"He's already the front man for a band—I think that's enough exposure."

"There's no such thing as too much publicity. You listen to me. We ensured Canada didn't acquire nuclear weapons. Have you seen the shitshow going on in the world?"

Of course I do. I watch the news every night and despair of our world. That's why I keep fighting. "The world is in a bad place."

"It's a good thing you don't have children—because what kind of world would you be leaving to them? On the other hand, perhaps if you had children, you might work harder to make things better."

That familiar knife in my chest twisted. The ache in my heart increased. *Let it go. It's not going to happen, and dwelling over it will only make you feel worse.* "I'll continue fighting, Mother. Whether or not I have children, I still believe in a cause greater than myself and my creature comforts." *There. That should shut her up. For now, at least.*

"Well, that's good. You do better, all right? And call Malik. Ask him to be more involved—not less."

"I will—"

The line went dead.

Ha! I'd been about to say that I'd *consider* it. Now I'd left her with the impression I actually would make the phone call. Well, her problem. If she had time to call and lecture, but not enough of her precious time to properly say *goodbye*, then that wasn't my issue.

Moses meowed.

His orange fur glowed in the illumination cast by the nightlight.

"I'll feed you, buddy. You were very patient."

He didn't like my parents. Well, I couldn't be certain he liked very many people as I rarely had people over. My parents had made the effort almost a year ago. After a very painful visit that lasted less than an hour, they'd departed and Moses had finally made an appearance. Smart cat. I'd have hidden if I could've.

You're forty years old, and you still haven't dealt with your parents or your issues surrounding them. You need therapy.

Well, probably that notion was a bit extreme. At the very least, I needed to stop trying to obtain their approval. Their praise. Even leaving my corporate job and moving to the nonprofit sector had little effect. Hadn't even moved the needle.

I snagged my dressing gown and shrugged it on over my pajamas. At least I'd managed to undress when I got home. Waking up after having slept in jeans and a button-down shirt was never fun—but I'd done it more times than I could count.

Moses ambled behind me as I made my way to the kitchen.

Yeah, we're going to be okay.

I never did get around to calling Malik Forestal.

Chapter Six

Malik

"Are you sure you don't want to come? It's going to be fun." I spoke into my phone as I walked from the parking garage across the street to Vancouver City Hall.

"Dude, your definition of *fun* and mine are wildly different. Seraphina invited me over to her place and I promise you, we're not going to be discussing policy and plans and zoning and... Uh..."

"They're discussing a new social housing project." I looked both way before crossing Cambie Street—even though I had the walk sign.

"Well, Vancouver needs more affordable housing." Something rustled in the background. "But what does that have to do with you?"

"The land they want to build on used to belong to the Indigenous tribes of the region."

"Dude, all the land belonged to the tribes—that's why we say we're on the unceded territory of the..."

I wasn't going to fill in the blanks. I loved that most government bodies recognized we were merely colonizers. My affinity with the

Indigenous community ran deep. I knew what it meant to be discriminated against for the color of my skin. The grievances of those native to this land ran much deeper, though. They needed my support. "I've made it to city hall. Wish me luck."

"Dude, whatever. Stay out of trouble, okay?" He cut the line before I had a chance to respond.

Probably just as well since he wouldn't have liked my answer.

I made my way to the room where the council was meeting. I slipped into a seat in the back row, noting at least four people on their phones in the gallery. Or what I supposed was the gallery. Although the room was large, the area for the public wasn't that big.

The lady who sat at the center of the room—and on an elevated platform—was the mayor. I hadn't voted for her. Not progressive enough, in my books. She'd done okay so far, so I'd given her the benefit of the doubt. Only a couple of the councilors sat in chairs, although I quickly realized some were attending the meeting virtually.

A bunch of procedural stuff happened—including evacuation procedures. This all felt unnecessary, but I supposed there must be a good reason for it. The mayor then gave the land dedication. *She said it too fast. She didn't give us time to reflect on what it means.* Moments later, she was on to business.

The first three items were boring as fuck. Renewal of some program that encouraged the construction of net-zero homes. Well, that was good. The rezoning of two adjacent lots so the developer could build a four-plex instead of the current two single-family homes. Increased densification. Sounded like a great idea. Vancouver's housing crunch was legendary, with one of the lowest vacancy rates in Canada. Anything we could do to increase densification was a good thing.

Finally, after what felt like forever, the proposal for the social housing came up. The councilors asked questions. The mayor peppered in a few. The developers clearly knew their stuff as they had answers for everything. What I wasn't hearing, though, was how they were going to be respectful of Indigenous people.

Is this even your fight? You're not Indigenous. You don't have a stake in this.

The project was to be in Kitsilano—a tonier neighborhood in the city.

With a lot of detractors. Person after person spoke—all NIMBY people. *Not in my backyard.* Well, where did they think people were going to live?

One particular lady got my hackles up. She kept going on and on about *those people*.

Finally, Spencer was called up. He went up to the lectern, put down his papers, and looked up toward the mayor. "Thank you, Mayor Johnson and council members. I am Spencer Wainright, and I'm the administrator for This Land is Ours. Our mission is to ensure Indigenous rights are respected and environmental protections are enacted. Normally, we focus on pipelines and other things detrimental to tribal lands. For too long, we haven't taken care of either the members of the community or the land on which we reside. I am speaking in favor of this new project. Of course we need more social housing. I want to ensure, however, that equity is involved. That—"

He glared at me as I nudged him aside.

"What he's trying to say is that although the amount of social housing in this project is good, it could be better. The developer's going to get rich off the at-market-rate units—so they can damn well build more units for the less advantaged."

A throat clearing behind me had me turning. I faced the woman who'd spoken vehemently against the proposal. "What's your problem? How does this affect you? People need a place to live."

"They can live on the east side." Her *where they belong* was completely implied in her statement.

"There's not enough housing on the east side. There's not enough housing anywhere. Why is it so wrong to give—"

"I'd like to see order." The mayor's words rang out.

I pivoted my attention back to her. "I was just saying—"

"Whomever you are, you're not on the speakers' list." The mayor glowered at me.

"But I just—" Even as I said the words, Spencer grabbed my arm with both of his hands and yanked me.

Hard.

"Hey, wait just—"

"No waiting. Apologies to you and council. We'll be leaving now."

"Very well." The mayor eyed her list. "Has everyone who wished to speak taken a turn?"

"Well, I haven't—" Again, Spencer pushed me away from the lectern.

"Do we need to call security?" The mayor appeared to be reaching for something.

"I'll go." I glared at Spencer. "Sorry." With that, I stormed out of the chamber. Righteous anger—and Spencer—followed me right out to 12th Avenue. I rounded on him. "What the fuck? I had everything under control."

His green eyes went wide. "What are you talking about? You had nothing under control. I had sound arguments and reasoning and was about to present some interesting findings—"

"More studies? More logic? You have to act with your heart, Spencer. Otherwise, people are just going to tune you out."

"Hey." He frowned. "People do not *tune me out*. I'll have you know I've presented before council before, and—"

"Did they vote the way you wanted to?"

The frown increased. "Not always—"

"Well, they sure as shit weren't going to this time either."

"You don't know that. I might've made a persuasive argument—if I hadn't been rudely interrupted."

I pursed my lips. "You always play it safe. You never risk anything. Real change isn't going to happen unless you put yourself on the line." I stepped into his space and put our faces mere inches apart. "I think you're chickenshit. You're afraid of being real about the struggles."

"That's bullshit, Malik. I'm in the fight every day. I might not be in people's faces—"

"But you should be. They should know about This Land is Ours. They should understand what the fight and struggle are all about. Too many people wander around this city...hell, this province..." I rubbed my forehead. "Hell, this country and even this planet. People don't get it."

"Some people get it." He held my gaze. "But there are better ways to get what you want than grandstanding and showboating."

"I wasn't doing either." God, he so didn't understand. "If you stand for nothing...if you speak out for nothing...then what's the point?"

"I was trying to speak." He gestured wildly toward the building. "You didn't give me a chance. I'd like to believe I could've made a persuasive argument. But you interrupted, and then I lost my turn. God, you're always thinking with—" He cut off.

"With what?" I was super interested in what he was thinking. Maybe I had cut him off—which would have been rude—but he was droning on and not getting to the point. Not imbuing the audience with the sense of urgency the situation required.

"With, I don't know, anything other than your brain. You're brave. Great. Fantastic. That doesn't move us forward. That doesn't help us achieve our goals. You need to understand that it's not about you. It's not about people doing what you think they should—"

"Wait a minute. I never said you should chain yourself to a bridge."

"Good, because I'm never going to do that. I'm a member of the bar of British Columbia in good standing. I'm not going to risk that for some harebrained, half-baked, stupid—"

"Don't call me stupid." I said the words low. Almost a growl. I could put up with a lot of shit and name calling—but stupid was a hard limit for me. The bully at my school would run around saying all Black kids were *stupid*. I reported it to a teacher, because I wasn't the only Black kid who was hurt, and the little shit denied it. The teacher took his side, of course, and I got a reputation as a snitch as well.

I might've eventually grown bigger than the bully, but his words and taunts never ended. He knew that I couldn't, as a Black kid, risk getting in a fight. Plus, he always had tons of friends and followers. I was one of the few Black kids in my school. I went to school with a rainbow of color, but the minority kids didn't always stick together.

Leaving high school had been the best day of my life.

Losing my parents had been the worst.

"I didn't call you stupid." Spencer pressed a hand to his temple. "Sometimes your ideas are..."

"Are what? Hey, are you okay?"

"I'm fine." He snapped that.

"Then what—"

He cut me off by launching himself at me, pulling me flush against him, and pressing his lips to mine. When I attempted to speak—whether to protest or encourage, I couldn't be certain—he thrust his tongue into my mouth. He grasped the back of my neck, lowered his head slightly, and then devoured me whole. His tongue sought the recesses of my mouth, even as his hands held me tight. Then those hands were meandering down my neck, to my chest, along my flank, then to my ass.

He pressed us closer.

I angled myself so our erect cocks brushed. Even through the layers of denim and khaki, I felt his arousal.

It matched my own.

The concept of consent flitted through my mind. How he hadn't asked. How I probably would've said no. How, if I had, I would've been missing out on all this.

I wrapped my arms around him to pull him even closer. So there wasn't a breath of wind that could pass between the two of us. Yet, the slightly rational side of my mind, pointed out we were standing on the steps of city hall. That anyone could walk by at any moment. The irrational side—the side that apparently drove Spencer nuts—truly didn't give a shit. I'd been attracted to him since the first moment I stormed into his office. I'd been pissed. Hell, I still was pissed. But none of that seemed to matter as he squeezed my ass.

Yeah, I wanted him. I wanted him so badly that I was willing to drag him behind a building and have my way with him. Would he be willing? Would he be interested? Was he a bottom or a top? This would be an important question to have an answer to because I always topped. I wasn't vers. I wasn't a switch. I liked what I liked, and I never deviated from that.

Hence the fact Creed and I were just friends. We'd been horny enough to contemplate trying to bottom for each other. In the end, though, neither of us had been willing to compromise. We were better off as friends.

And why the fuck was I thinking about Creed while this infuriating man had his tongue down my throat, and his hands planted firmly on my ass?

No idea.

I tried to refocus on him. I didn't know what would make him feel good, but I was certainly willing to try. Within the boundaries of decency, of course. I'd taken Mama Murthi's admonishment to heart—I was not going to risk getting arrested and not being able to perform in Black Rock. *If* Rocktoberfest ever came calling. I had my doubts.

Spencer pulled back abruptly, then pushed off against me.

I nearly fell backward. "Hey."

He shook his head. "I'm sorry. That was... And you were... We shouldn't..." His pupils nearly eclipsed his entire irises as he gestured. Something between the two of us—if I could make sense of his rapid movement.

"Look, can we talk?"

"I have to go." He turned and fled.

Like an idiot, I stood there with my mouth gaping. Because what had happened was both super hot and super weird. I didn't care that he hadn't asked. I was someone who could stand up for myself. *I hope he hasn't done that to someone in the past who didn't want it. Or doesn't do it in the future with someone who also isn't welcoming of that overture.*

But that fucking amazing, awesome, brilliant kiss. Man, could he kiss. My lips still tingled where he'd pressed against me. My rock-hard cock wasn't happy about the lack of options. Much as I wanted to rub one out—to clear up the ache—I wasn't going to do that either in public or even in my car. Nope, driving home with a hopefully deflating cock was about the best I could do, given the circumstances.

Several people exited city hall.

The NIMBY woman came up to me and shook her fists. "Look what you've done." Then she marched off.

A gentleman approached me next. "I'm not certain you can take all—or any—of the credit. But the project was green-lit. So that's good news." He slapped me on the back. "Quite a show you put on in there." Then he took off.

I'll watch the council minutes when they post. I needed to see if I'd been as rude as Spencer claimed. I also needed to see for certain that the project would go ahead. And if any Indigenous input would be sought. Likely not, but I could hope.

I adjusted my jeans, so I was slightly more comfortable, and headed to my SUV. So a good day...right?

Hard to tell. Reading Spencer was impossible—or damn close to it— so I had only my gut reaction to go by.

My gut—and my cock—said, *more, more, more.*

Interesting to see if I listened to my brain, which said *danger, danger, danger.*

Chapter Seven

Spencer

*H*oly fuck.

Did I just...?

Did he just...?

How is it we're not in a bed excising each other from our systems?

I couldn't answer any of those questions. Or attempts at questions. In truth, I had no idea what had just fucking happened. As I cycled back to my condo, the reality of what I'd just done sank in.

I'd kissed a guy.

Okay, no big deal. I was gay, he was—at the very least—bi.

We'd been in public.

Nothing against PDAs. They might not have been my thing, but Malik clearly had no issues with...getting involved.

I didn't have his permission. Didn't ask for it. Didn't wait for it. Didn't stop until way, way, way too fucking late in the process.

Yep. Had to own that one. Even the memory had my gut churning. I was a lawyer, for fuck's sake. If anyone understood the concept of consent, it would be lawyers and members of law enforcement. I might not deal in criminal law, but I'd taken the classes. Had seen up close what victimization looked like.

Malik...

Well, he hadn't appeared victimized. In fact, he'd been the one to haul us closer together. His tongue had parried with mine. He'd thrust his erection against me. We couldn't have been closer. Hell, we'd been downright indecent.

And I would've stopped in a heartbeat if he'd asked me to. If he'd shown any sign of not being into what we were doing.

You know that doesn't matter. Try and justify it all you want...it won't make you any less guilty.

That knowledge sat in the pit of my stomach as I considered going through a drive-through for some dinner or something. I'd eaten some yogurt and strawberries before the meeting because I hadn't wanted to feel weighted down and I didn't want to feel hungry either.

Now? Ravenous. Like I could masticate an entire cow all on my own. Added to the queasy feeling and everything felt off-kilter.

I locked up my bike in front of the A&W drive-through on Broadway as I considered my options. The veggie burger, of course, but then... Onion rings. I deserved a side of onion rings. I added a root beer, made it a combo, and six minutes later, I was cycling home with my meal shoved into messenger bag.

Home these days was complicated.

When I worked at BioVale, with my very lucrative corporate salary, I'd bought a nice condo in the west end. I'd enjoyed the nightlife on Davie Street. I'd driven a nice car. I'd also donated to charities and had supported friends who were involved in politics and social justice. Hands-off, though. I couldn't risk my job.

I rolled my eyes as I locked my bike to the wall by my parking space in my Mount Pleasant condo. I jogged up to the third floor and let myself into my rather tiny unit. Sighing, I dropped my keys onto my little table in the front hall. I toed off my shoes and headed to my high-top table. I eased myself onto a bar stool as Moses leapt up to join me. "Shoo."

He plopped down on the stool across from me and eyed me.

"Onions are bad for cats." I sorted my drink, burger, and onion rings. "I'm not sharing."

The cat blinked. Innocently. Then indolently.

I unwrapped the burger and tore off a sliver of the veggie goodness. "Just one bite."

He snagged it off my finger.

I eyed the finger, decided I was too tired to get up to wash my hand, and dug into my food with relish. I hadn't realized how tired I was until this moment.

A couple of times, Moses tried to steal more food.

In resignation, I tore off a tiny strip of lettuce and let him go to town. By the time he'd finished it, I'd polished off the burger, onion rings, and about half my root beer.

I gazed around my one-bedroom condo. I could've fit two of these into my old place in the west end. With room to spare. I'd also been on the twenty-first floor with floor-to-ceiling windows facing English Bay.

Here? Third floor—the top—with a nice view of the back alley and the building behind us. I had a *casual wave* relationship with the neighbor behind me. At least her unit faced south and got some semblance of sun. Mine faced north and was in darkness all day.

That said, when I had the migraines, I was happy to shut my black-out blinds, crawl into bed, and pray for death.

Huh.

I'd been okay today. Given how rough the last few days had been, that was saying something.

Moses eyed me.

I balled up my wrappers, put them in the paper bag, and tossed it into the recycling bin.

Well, attempted to. The shot—which was only a few feet—went long.

Moses leapt from his stool and tore across the condo. Clearly, he'd decided the paper bag was a new version of a ball, and he intended to have fun with it. Either that, or he was going to try to suck the residual grease from the paper. Not possible and, uh, gross.

Entirely something a cat would do.

With yet another weary sigh, I headed over to my desk. I plopped into my chair and tapped my laptop.

It awoke and demanded a password.

I obliged it and soon the background of Moses popped up. I smiled, as I always did. No matter how horrible or crazy my day was, I could always count on some sanity when I got home.

Moses jumped onto my desk and attempted to walk on the keyboard.

"Hey." I gently shoved him off.

He glared.

"Oh shit." I rose and headed to the kitchen.

Damn cat was hard on my heels.

"I'm sorry. I meant to come home before the council meeting, but I got caught responding to emails, and then it was time to go to the meeting." I offered this excuse to a cat who truly didn't give a shit—just as long as I fed him. "You know, you have perfectly good kibble right here." I nudged the bowl with my toe.

He sat next to the bowl and stared at me, clearly conveying his absolute disinterest in the food. He wanted the wet stuff, and he wanted it right now.

"Yeah, yeah." I put the plate down with the perfectly portioned wet food.

Without even bothering to thank me, he dug in.

Wearily, I headed back to the computer.

Hesitantly, I checked the website of the developer of the social housing project.

We have received Vancouver Council approval...

Well, fuck me sideways. That definitely hadn't been there when I'd checked a few hours ago.

I checked the local news website, and an article confirming the go-ahead had just appeared a few minutes ago. I scanned it and...

My heart sank.

First, I located a quote from that busybody who truly would be no worse off. Her home was several blocks from the proposed site, and her *enjoyment* wasn't going to be affected. If she was bothered by all the people who couldn't afford to buy two-million-dollar homes, she could suck my dick.

Gross. Just...gross.

The reporter made it clear not everyone in the neighborhood was against the development and some saw the densification as a good thing. Also a tacit acknowledgement it might make the area marginally less white.

What really caused my stomach to go into freefall was the paragraph about the *interruption* of council proceedings by none other than Malik Forestal.

Jesus Fucking Christ.

Now, my name didn't appear, so hopefully the connection to This Land is Ours would remain hidden. I scanned the comments after the article, and nothing had popped up yet.

Yet.

Moses leapt onto the desk.

Absentmindedly, I petted him.

His purrs soothed me.

My phone rang.

At ten-twenty in the evening. Not a good sign.

Bonnie.

"Hey." Because answering with my standard professional greeting was just so not happening. I put it on speaker phone and dropped it onto the desk.

"Congratulations."

"Thanks...?"

"You don't sound happy. Come to think of it though, you never sound happy."

"Hey."

"What?"

"I might resemble that remark."

"There's a moment of self-awareness."

"Yep." Then I rubbed my eyes. "I am capable of them."

"You weren't mentioned."

"I never got to speak."

"Malik was mentioned."

I sighed.

"Right. Well, get some sleep. I'll see you in the morning." She cut the call.

Probably didn't want to hear my gripe. I put the computer into sleep mode, shooed the cat off the desk, and headed to my bedroom.

I stripped, put my clothes in the hamper, then I headed into the bathroom. I set the shower spray for the perfect temperature and got in. *Shit. I closed the bathroom door, right?* Poking my head out, and finding the door shut, I relaxed.

Moses had a habit of trying to jump into the shower with me. He didn't like water, and so usually scratched me a few times before I managed to get him out. Cat didn't have a knack for learning lessons he didn't want to learn. Hence the reason he was never allowed outside. I could totally see him trying to jump off the balcony. He had a cat patio that allowed him to go outside without actually letting him free. He was, of course, disgruntled. And also still alive—so I took that for a win.

I washed my hair and tried to put images of Malik out of my mind.

Which proved impossible. Tonight, he'd worn dark-blue jeans, a button-down white shirt, and—of all things—cowboy boots. *He looked both respectable and a little bad ass with the boots. Do rock stars normally wear boots like that?*

Come to that, why did it matter?

Because you want a repeat of that kiss. You want to drag him to bed and let him have his wicked way with you. You'd been so tempted to get to your knees, right there in front of city hall and—

I tried not to continue that thought.

But the kiss... Yeah, that had been... Spectacular? Amazing? Noteworthy?

Exact words failed me. Which, as a lawyer, was a bad thing.

My cock stiffened as I remembered how good it'd felt to brush against him. How much I'd wanted skin on skin. How I'd dominated a kiss I hadn't even obtained consent to initiate.

I grasped my shaft. Whether to try to stop the erection or to prolong it, I wasn't entirely certain.

In the end, my body demanded satisfaction. A completion to what had started earlier this evening. Some kind of relief that only jerking off would bring. Bringing the image of Malik to my mind, and a couple of rough tugs, found me coming hard and fast.

I braced one hand against the wall while I milked myself through an intense climax. For once, I didn't worry about using too much water. Didn't worry about how much energy I was using and what that cost would be. Instead, I luxuriated. I drifted. I soared.

In the end, I cleaned myself up, ensured all the cum was down the drain, and got out of the shower. As I looked at myself in the mirror, I winced.

Not your greatest moment, Wainright. Did you really accomplish anything?

Perhaps one thing. Maybe now, I could get Malik Forestal out of my system once and for all.

Or so I told myself.

Chapter Eight

Malik

Mama Murthi glared at me over her cup of tea.

"What?" I had to feign ignorance. That might at least buy me some time. I was better off just leaving, but she'd said she wanted to talk to me. So I sat in her kitchen on a rainy afternoon, waiting for her message from on high.

"Creed showed me the concert footage."

Of Grindstone.

At Rocktoberfest.

The quality hadn't been great and, of course, the sound had been hard to hear. But I'd watched the footage dozens of times.

Mesmerized, I'd followed each song carefully—trying to figure out why they put each song in the order they had. Trying to divine how they were so successful while Razor Made languished in near-obscurity. Then they'd brought the house down with their new song, "In Another Life". At the end, their lead singer Axel, had looked out into the crowd. Someone had shouted something at him, and he replied they were all taken. *Does that mean he's with his teacher? Are they going to come out?*

Axel and Ed, the bassist, had cultivated personas of men who liked women. They were certainly seen with enough of them. Now Ed was with documentary filmmaker Thornton, and Axel apparently was with his former high school teacher, Hugo.

In a way, that blew my mind. Otherwise, it simply confirmed someone could come out as gay and lose almost no fans. Since I'd always been out, I'd worried we might not get fans in the first place. We had some loyal ones, though.

Mama continued to stare at me.

I continued to sip my coffee. "Did you enjoy the show?"

"Big place. Lots of noise. Disreputable."

Two years ago, a rocker had died of an OD. That had cast a pall over the event and, even though I hadn't been there, I'd heard. "I'm not disreputable. Grindstone isn't disreputable."

"My friend Renee is best friends with Hugo Threadgold."

I wracked my brains. "Axel's former teacher? The one who's back in his life? The guy from that kiss video?"

She arched an eyebrow. "Ah, so you do pay attention. Good to know. Yes, Axel and Hugo are...circling each other."

"What does that even mean?"

"You need to find a nice boy and settle down. Renee said Ed and Thornton are married. It looks like Axel might get together with Hugo. Meg and Big Mac are together. Even Songbird might be with someone. But that's hush-hush."

My eyes widened. "How do you know all this?" I snapped my fingers. "Right, friend of a friend. I won't ask how you know each other."

"She's a teacher. I represented one of her students in a court case. She gave testimony. Darn good stuff. Got the kid acquitted—which was good, because the girl hadn't done what she was accused of." She took another sip of her tea.

I tried to digest her news. I was single—as were Creed, Reese, and Freddie. We took our music seriously, and that meant no permanent attachments. Didn't mean all of us didn't have hookup apps on our phone. Well, except Reese. I could never be certain where she found partners for her *liaisons*—her word, not mine. She didn't brag about her conquests, but she often smiled and said she was *satisfied*. I took that to mean well-sated. "What are you saying?"

"You all need to find permanent partners. People who will support you in your music endeavor, but who will also keep your egos in check."

My knee-jerk reaction was to argue. I didn't need a partner. I didn't need a keeper. I certainly didn't need a husband. "I think you do a great job at keeping our egos in check." I rose, pressed a kiss to her cheek, dumped the dregs of my coffee down the drain, put the mug in the dishwasher, and waved my farewell.

"You be a good boy." She wagged her finger at me.

I pressed my hand to my chest, imitating being wounded. "I'm always a good boy."

"Ha." She barked out her laugh just as Papa Murthi shuffled into the kitchen. The married couple were almost the same age. Butt while Mama was spry, intense, and wicked smart, Papa had lost a step or two in the couple of years I'd known him. He shuffled more, spoke less, and he wasn't always coherent.

Mama and Creed didn't appear ready to acknowledge the change. I couldn't force them to face reality. Hopefully Papa was getting good medical care, and a doctor was following him closely.

I gave his arm a squeeze.

He met my gaze, frowned, then smiled. "You're such a good boy."

Mama barked out more laughter as I took my leave. I drove straight to Spencer's office and presented myself to Bonnie with as little attitude as possible.

She gave me the once-over.

"I just want to talk to him."

"I'm not certain he wants to talk to you." She had her hand on her hip.

Brushing past her would be easy enough—but that likely meant laying hands on her and no way was I going to do that. "I promise to be good."

She laughed.

"No, truly. I can be a good guy. I can behave."

She narrowed her eyes. "Do you even understand what we're fighting for?"

"For Indigenous tribes to have their ancestral lands recognized as their own and for the environment to be protected. Of course, I understand."

"Do you also see that it's mostly white folks fighting for this?"

"Are you saying I can't join you because I'm not white? Because I'm Black?"

"No. You misunderstand. We welcome everyone. But we also ask them to abide by rules and use decorum."

Ah. Now we're getting somewhere.

"Polite and decorous doesn't always get the job done." I gestured to the photo of the founder or the organization. Maude Ransom. "She wasn't always polite and decorous."

"And she never accomplished as much in life as she wanted. She changed some hearts and minds—but not all. Even she recognized her limitations. Her desire, when she passed, was that her legacy be carried on. That work be done in her name."

"Okay." I frowned. "But you need money, right?"

"We're surviving. That said, additional funds are always a good thing—as long as they're not the proceeds of crime or something."

I waved my hand as if to wave off her suggestion I might do anything untoward. "I'm a saint."

"You're anything but." Spencer's dry tone had me pivoting to find him close behind me.

I didn't even sense him. He must move stealthily.

"What can I do for you, Mr. Forestal? I'm really quite busy, and—"

"Razor Made wants to create an anthem for This Land is Ours. To use as you see fit. Maybe even to overlay a video you create that explains your mission. Or maybe you pull it out at your next rally. Or—"

He held up his hand. "I get the picture and am not interested, Mr. Forestal. Thank you for dropping by and please attempt not to get in trouble again—"

"Hey." I frowned. "That thing you supported got approved."

"No thanks to you." He frowned right back. "Perhaps the project was always going to be green-lit. But your impassioned speech—"

I rolled my eyes.

"—didn't make much sense and upset the mayor. And got attention from the local press."

Ah. So that's the problem—he's jealous. "I'm sure if you contact the media that you can get your name in—"

"That's not the point."

"That's always the point." Bonnie stepped between the two of us as she said the words. "I'm going to make this clear." She gazed at me. "You're going to be rational, calm, and polite."

Pretty much exactly what Mama Murthi was demanding of me.

Bonnie turned to Spencer. "And you've going to be rational, calm, and polite."

I puffed out my chest. Ha. She saw him as highhanded and rude as well. Score one for me.

"I'm always polite and—" Spencer cut off as the petite woman glared at him. She was almost half-a-foot shorter than me, and I was a few good inches shorter than him. The difference between the two of them was almost a foot.

And yet, clearly, Bonnie considered herself in charge around here. I didn't smile. Well, I didn't smile too much. I liked watching her put her boss—the arrogant Spencer Wainright—in his place.

His green eyes flashed as his gaze traveled from Bonnie to me and back again. Finally, he shrugged. "I'll listen to what he has to say. If I don't like it, though, then I have the right to show him to the door."

"Well, I suppose." Bonnie pointed her finger at him. "But I think you need to listen to him. He's worth paying attention to."

Her words warmed me because compliments about me were rare. Creed occasionally remembered. Reese was decent. Freddie was useless, and Mama Murthi only praised me when I'd done a really good job. So, despite Spencer's vague acquiescence to allow me entry—for at least a few minutes—it was the beginning of either a thawing in our relationship or the entire demise.

I just couldn't figure out which it was based on what had just happened.

Chapter Nine

Spencer

Normally, my office felt spacious—with my ergonomic chair behind my large desk, two chairs across from it, as well as the sofa I spent far too much time laying on because of the fucking migraines.

With Malik in my space, however, it felt claustrophobic. Like I could barely breathe without inhaling his scent. Sandalwood? Maybe? Not something that appeared to trigger my fucking head—so I'd take that for a win. "Would you like to take a seat?"

"How's your head?"

My gaze shot to his.

"Kind of obvious the last time I was here that something was happening. I mean, I'm glad you didn't have a seizure or something—that would've been scary. But you went all white and kept pressing your hand to your temple."

Had I? I'd no memory of any of that. Not entirely surprising, however. Often, once the aura—and then the pain—struck, everything became fuzzy. Sometimes just around the edges and sometimes, like that day, every fucking thing. "I'm okay, thank you for asking."

"But you need to keep your stress level down, right? Blood pressure and all that?"

My eyebrows shot up.

"My best friend's baby sister. Creed's taught me how to read the signs. I mean, when there are signs. Sometimes it just hits her hard and nothing helps. She's on this new drug. The damn thing's amazing—"

"I'm allergic to an ingredient."

"Aw shit, that sucks." He cocked his head—as if trying to get a read on me. "Anyway, I recognized some of the symptoms. I kind of figured you didn't want me to see you like that, so I told Bonnie you needed help and then I left. I admit to feeling a little guilty." He scrunched his nose. "Okay, like, a lot. But I was also still mad about the interview you did with CNC."

I let out a long exhalation. "I could have been...more diplomatic."

"Yeah? Because I'm not all about the clicks and likes. I mean, those are nice, and I get a bit of a hit, but I'm more interested in the comments. Do people understand why I'm doing what I'm doing? Do they listen to the lyrics and get the message? I'm really good at lyrics, by the way. Creed sucks, although if he gives me a good story, then I can tell it." He rolled his eyes. "My point—and I do have one—is that I'm good at composing lyrics. Freddie, our keyboardist, and Reese, our bassist, do most of the scoring. Between the four of us, we make a good team."

"I've heard your stuff, and I won't disagree. Just not clear why you're here today." He scrunched his nose.

"Mrs. Murthi said I had to come and apologize."

Again, his eyebrows shot up. "Mrs. Murthi is related to Creed?"

"Yeah, his mom. And she sort of considers herself my mom, and since pissing off my mom is the last thing I'd ever want to do, I'm here to apologize to you as well."

"That's...big of you."

"Mama Murthi is a force to be reckoned with. If I want to continue eating samosas and French fries at her table, then I do what I'm told."

The image of samosas with French fries slammed into my mind, and my stomach rumbled.

Malik cocked his head.

"Skipped breakfast. I had a conference call with some donors back east. Crazy early for me, but midmorning for them. They're making the contributions, so they get to set the meeting times."

"Not if that means you're skipping meals."

"Truly, I meant to get up earlier to make myself some food. But I was queasy and hadn't slept well last night—"

"Because of me?"

I squinted.

"Because I ruined the council meeting for you? I mean, they voted for the development you went to support, so I don't think you should be entirely pissed."

I glared.

He stood taller. Still a few inches shorter than me, but from this distance, our gazes were almost level.

"Your behavior—" Then, "Hey!."

He had my arm and was propelling me through the door to the outer offices. "We can call for delivery, or we can go out. I know this great café around the corner."

"The Garden Strathcona?"

"Yep. Let's go."

"I'll go voluntarily if you'll release me."

He met my gaze. "I think you like when I touch you."

Heat rushed to my cheeks. Memories from last night—which I'd conveniently forgotten—raced back to my mind. My cock, previously uninterested, perked up at his somewhat domineering tone. *This isn't like you—you don't like to be bossed around.*

Depends who's doing the bossing.

Well...that was possibly true. I'd never met someone so...magnetic as Malik. Part of me was willing to submit to anything just to see how far he'd take things. "The Garden Strathcona's a bit on the expensive side."

"I can afford it. Let's go." He released my arm, then gestured me to head out.

I dropped my messenger bag—full of papers, but nothing else—onto my desk. Then I followed him.

Malik was smiling at Bonnie. "What can I get you?"

My assistant beamed. "I'd love a kale Caesar salad. How lovely of you to offer."

I rolled my eyes, but ensured no one saw me. For Malik's wallet's sake, I was glad Bonnie was the only one in the office today.

He caught sight of me and gestured for me to follow.

I waved to Bonnie and hustled to keep up. Thank God I hadn't removed my coat, because the cold wind coming in off Coal Harbor was pretty brutal. The gray clouds overhead promised rain, and my head was giving off the super-early warning signals that, if I wasn't careful, I might get hit with a migraine. "Are we eating at the restaurant or back at the office?"

Malik, who'd been striding down East Pender Street toward Hawkes Avenue, slowed his pace. "I figured we could do takeout and eat in your office. You seem to like to be in control—of some things—and your office gives you that power." With those simple words, he continued the trek—turning north on Hawkes and heading toward Hastings Street.

My mind stuttered. *Is he right? Do I derive a power trip by having people in my office? That feels a little farfetched. But also perhaps true?* "How do you know about the café?"

"The recording studio where I work is just a few blocks from here. When we're not ordering cheap delivery pizza, we're often ordering something completely healthy. The café food hits the spot." He eyed me. "I can be an adult."

"You take your samosas with a side of French fries." Said somewhat dryly.

He barked out a laugh. "Yeah, Mama Murthi used to have the same opinion. I often include a side of steamed vegetables, so she's willing to overlook the fries."

We hit Hastings Street and headed east the half block until we arrived at the café.

Heavenly scents assailed me as I stepped inside. Again, because the store favored organics and natural flavors, the scents didn't trigger me. Certainly if it'd been a risk, I wouldn't have ventured near here. Other places around here were on a hard *no* list. If I wanted something, I either had it delivered or had Bonnie run out—with me paying for her meal, of course.

"We can eat here, but it's almost lunchtime. We might not want to make Bonnie wait." Better than admitting that yes, I did feel more in control in my office.

"I vote for not making the lady wait." He gestured for me to place my order first.

As I approached the counter, he pressed against my back. "My treat."

A shiver ran up and down my spine. "I prefer—"

"Next time, you can pay."

Which, of course, implied there would be a next time.

"What can I get for you?" A lovely woman with shining dark-brown eyes met my gaze.

"Uh…" Sheesh. I'd eaten here dozens of times. Did I feel adventurous or…? Nope. Better to go safe. "I'll have the simple grilled cheese. To go. And a kale Caesar salad to go." See? I could remember Bonnie's order.

I advanced even as Malik kept his hand on my lower back. I didn't need steadying…but I also didn't try to move away.

"I'll have the coconut curry bowl."

"Great. Right away." She rang up our order.

My companion entered a tip, then tapped his card.

"Malik, lovely to see you." Together we turned to see a gentleman in a white shirt and crisp khaki pants.

We turned, and Malik offered a wide grin. "Hey Ty, how are you?"

"I'm doing well." The men shook hands. "You don't happen to have more of your CDs, do you? I think we're down to our last one."

"Oh, wow. Yeah, I have some in my SUV. I can drop them off in a couple of hours?"

"Great. I'll e-transfer you the money for the ones we've sold. Almost as popular as Grindstone." He winced. "I wasn't supposed to say that, was I?"

I considered it a little rude, but Malik's grin widened. "To have my name uttered in the same sentence as Grindstone is a big deal. Oh, Ty, this is Spencer."

No explanation. Just…Spencer.

Ty held out his hand. "I've seen you here before. I wondered if you lived in the neighborhood."

"My office is in a house on East Pender."

"Spencer runs This Land is Ours." Malik stood a little taller. "We're discussing whether or not Razor Made will write an anthem for the group."

Ty nodded, clearly approving of the idea.

Maybe you should let me have my say before you go announcing it to the world? Alas, I was learning that wasn't how Malik operated. He spoke first and only later reflected on the potential consequences.

"That sounds like it would be a good fit." Ty turned his attention to me. "We don't advertise that we sell Malik's CDs, but we like to support local artisans. Local artistes."

I wasn't certain what to make of the man. He was medium-height, slender, with a lovely face, luminescent blue eyes, and high cheek-bones. His midnight-black hair flopped in just *that* way. Something I could never manage and therefore kept mine short. "That's good of you."

"Well, I'm a huge Razor Made fan." Ty offered a sheepish grin.

"They are unique." I hadn't gone through their entire catalogue, but I could see how this oasis of calm and paradise wasn't a place to play hard rock music.

"Mr. Forestal? I have your order."

We pivoted our attention back to the food counter where a canvas bag with what appeared to be our food containers rested.

"Thanks." Malik grinned. "I'll bring the bag back when I return with the CDs."

"That would be appreciated." The young woman beamed.

Is everyone enthralled with this guy? Sheesh.

Admit it...you find him sexy as well.

Yeah, but—

Didn't you jerk off to his image while in the shower last night?

Heat raced to my face. Luckily, no one seemed interested in me. The entire focus was on Malik.

He snagged the canvas tote. "Thanks for this—I'll be back before you close."

"Can't wait." Ty gave a little wave.

"Looking forward to it." Our server beamed.

Malik nodded, finally appeared to notice me, and came to stand by my side. "Shall we go?"

"Sure." I was a forty-year-old man who wasn't going to feel hurt because the guy I was with was super popular and, for a few moments, appeared to have forgotten my existence.

We headed back onto Hastings Street, this time heading west.

"Those are storm clouds." Malik switched the bag to his right hand so he could place his left at the small of my back.

Admit it...you like this side of him.

We still hadn't discussed the parameters of touch. Given I'd thrown myself at him last night—and he'd reciprocated, or at least returned, the affection—it seemed a safe bet that he wasn't concerned about us getting up close and personal.

"How do you know they're storm clouds?" For all my migraine-suffering days, I rarely gave the type of cloud any consideration. Clouds meant a change in weather. I gave forecasts far more weight—barometric pressure, humidity, and all that shit.

"I, uh, did really well in cloud class."

I nearly stopped walking, but we had the light to cross Hawkes Avenue, so I kept moving. "There's a cloud class? How did I miss that?"

"The benefits of a classical education." He said the words even as he directed me to continue south on Hawkes toward Pender.

"What are you talking about? Did you go to some special school for violin prodigies?"

He snorted. "My father would've loved that. No, I went to a regular school—at least my mom supported me on that. Still, one of the most exclusive high schools in Vancouver, though. Excellent academic achievement was a requirement of my father's. I was near the top in every class."

I caught a glance of a wince.

Still, he continued on. "Clouds were in grade school and, I admit, I found them endlessly fascinating. For a kid like me, whose mind was always wandering, the ability to just lie quietly and watch the clouds roll by was a treat. Those moments calmed my mind. So yes, I got one hundred percent in our unit on clouds. I didn't do as well in the dissection class in high school biology." He shivered.

I leaned a little closer, even as we turned onto Pender. "I hated that class as well."

He chuckled. "Glad to hear you're not perfect. I had wondered."

Asking him to explain that comment was on the tip of my tongue when we arrived at the house which, of course, doubled as an office. We'd had to obtain special bylaw permitting to allow this, and we had to make several upgrades, including a wheelchair ramp at the back of the building so we'd be accessible. I had no issues with that, but the renovations had cost money. Everything cost money.

Breathe.

"I should probably take my migraine-prevention pills." Admitting that level of frailty hurt, but the weather forecaster had predicted rain this afternoon. One of the reasons I hadn't biked to work.

"Great. I'll give Bonnie her salad, then join you. If that's all right."

Our gazes met as we walked up the short flight of stairs. "Uh, yeah, that would be fine."

Seriously? Did you just use the word fine? Still, I put on a brave smile and walked into the main office area. I waved to Bonnie as I headed into my office. I didn't like Malik knowing about my migraines—but he'd have likely sussed out the information eventually—but I didn't exactly keep them a secret. I'd hoped leaving my high-powered, high-stress corporate job would've alleviated some of them. Except working in the not-for-profit sector had proved to be equally as stressful. Just in a different way.

That, and my triggers hadn't changed—weather, strong chemical scents, certain foods, as well as about half-a-dozen other things. Including stress.

I popped two pills, then washed them down with some lukewarm water. *Hope that staves off the worst of it.*

Now...

What the fuck was I going to do about Malik Fucking Forestal?

Chapter Ten

Malik

I wasn't certain whether I should've brought up his migraines. Whether in relation to the storm clouds, or even at all. He was a grown man—nearly a decade and a half older than me—he could bloody well manage his headaches on his own.

Only, after watching Abrianna suffer for the first year I knew her—and then the year migraine-free after that—I didn't want Spencer to be in any more pain than absolutely necessary. I didn't know all his triggers, of course, but if Creed's sister's experiences were similar to Spencer's, storms were a big part of them. Possibly everything else as well.

Well, except likely not hormones and periods. TMI, frankly, but Abri shared liberally. To prepare me for being a good boyfriend if I ever dated a woman who got migraines. Who knew all that prep would be used toward a guy with the same affliction?

He sat in his chair as I wandered in.

"Bonnie said she'd bring us a couple of glasses of water. I said I could do it, but—"

Even as I said the words, the efficient woman came in with two tall glasses of ice water. She put them on coasters on Spencer's desk, gave me an extra-special smile, and then sauntered out of the office. Her "thanks for the salad," was barely audible as she closed the door behind her.

I met Spencer's gaze and blinked.

"She's efficient. There's no two ways about it. The nice woman who worked here before...wasn't. But she was a holdover from Maude's days. Oh, thank you."

He smiled a little shyly as I handed him his wrapped sandwich.

"I convinced her to take early retirement. Bonnie was the first person I interviewed for the job. I saw six others that day but none came close to impressing me the way she did. She came from the not-for-profit sector and was looking to reorient herself after a bad breakup—with the charity she worked for. Things had, in her words, *gone off the rails*. She made it clear if our focus ever wavered, she'd jump ship."

"Oh." I dropped onto the sofa, pulled out my bowl and fork, and started to stir. "So, is that why you're worried about me? That I might, I don't know, upset your apple cart? Which is a weird expression, but my mother used it all the time. *Behave, Malik. Don't upset the apple cart, Malik. Wait until your father gets home, Malik.*" I shivered. "That one was pretty effective—my father was...a difficult man. I never wanted to disappoint him."

"Was he the reason you played violin?"

I scrunched my nose. "Yes and no." I took a mouthful of food.

Spencer cocked his head.

I rushed to chew, and then swallow, my food. "We had a grand piano in the house. From a really early age, I'd sit at it and play tunes. I'd even make things up. Clearly, I had a gift neither parent did. But my father wanted more than just a piano prodigy. He considered that too...common. Even for a young Black boy. So, he hired the symphony conductor who took me through just about every instrument out there. For some reason, the violin fit. My father then found the most qualified instructor in the city to take over the tutelage." I shrugged. "When it comes to musical instruments, I'm a quick study. Don't get me wrong—I enjoyed the violin very much. Just...the opportunities to compose pieces didn't come often, and they weren't exciting. Truthfully, I just love rock music."

"Well, thank you for explaining that."

"I'm not certain I did. Once I showed an aptitude for violin, my father decided I needed to be a prodigy. The youngest to do everything. Even the best at everything. Now, I wasn't...other kids before me had broken the new ground in those respects. That said, I was showcased at an early age." I took another bite of food.

"Because of your talent?" He bit into his sandwich.

I swallowed. "Partly. Also, because I was a little Black kid. We're not as common in Vancouver as in other parts of Canada like Toronto. And where I went to school? I was pretty much on my own."

"Ouch."

He held my gaze with those mesmerizing green eyes. Eyes that made me want to tell him everything. Like where I lived, how life had been as a kid— all the shit I'd gone through.

"Yet you gave all that up."

"I suppose." I stirred my food. "I carried on at first, after my parents died. I wanted to make my dad proud. Eventually, though, I realized everything I was doing was for him—and he wasn't even here to see it. Either to praise or to criticize. Which, I freely admit, he did way more of one than the other." *More criticism and less praise. Obviously.* I didn't want Spencer to feel sorry for me—but I did want him to understand where I'd come from and why I was the way I was.

"What made you quit entirely?"

"I woke up one morning, looked at myself in the mirror, and acknowledged in no way could I play the violin in an orchestra for the next forty years and feel anything but a dull ache and a sense of loss. Yes, my father pushed me into it. Yes, I did it for him. I also did it for myself. I'm a competitive person, and I wanted to be the best. The best was studying music at the University of British Columbia and then joining the symphony." I shrugged. "That was all pretty straightforward. We'd talked about me taking guest first chairs at other orchestras. That would've eventually happened."

"But you quit."

"That day I decided. I had six more performances to go. They were tortuous because I'd tendered my resignation. I kept thinking *what if I've made the wrong decision? What if I'm fucking up my life?*" I shrugged yet again, trying to find the right words. "The director of the orchestra said I'd always be welcome back, but that felt hollow. I'd be starting from scratch. Yet, I knew." I took another bite.

"Knew?"

I swallowed. "That I'd made the right decision. I had an old acoustic guitar I pulled out of storage. I started playing around with it. Once I'd left the orchestra entirely, I bought an electric guitar and amp, and sheet music for hundreds of songs. I locked myself in my basement studio for a month and played until my fingers bled. By the end, though, I had a sense of who I was and what I wanted. I started going to shows around town. Dive bars, night clubs—anywhere I could find live music. I caught Creed playing drums with a truly horrific group. I mean…" I shuddered.

Spencer grinned. "Apparently that didn't stop you."

"Well, the singer was atrocious, the bassist kept fucking up the rhythm, and the keyboardist must've been high on something."

"Why do you say that?"

"Because he was literally playing the wrong song."

"Oh." Spencer cocked his head as if trying to work it out in his mind.

I wanted to assure him that whatever he came up with, the reality had been infinitely worse.

"Yeah, that wouldn't work."

"Nope. But the drummer held the band together. I approached him that night and asked if he was interested in joining me. I had zero cred, nothing to recommend myself except an amazing rehearsal space in my basement as well as the balls to proposition a guy who was still coated in sweat from the set he'd just done with his current band."

"And?"

"He was in my basement the next afternoon. By the time we found Freddie for keyboards and Reese for bass, we had a pile of songs. We had to play some pretty dicey places at first, but we worked our way up. My job working at a recording studio introduced me to some amazing people. I convinced some of them to take a chance on us. Our first album came out in April, and we've already got songs ready to go for the next one." I shoved another forkful of food in my mouth. Curry truly was one of my all-time favorite flavors. Had been even before Creed had brought me to his home to meet Mama Murthi.

"And you have grander ambitions? Sorry, I keep asking questions while you're eating."

I swallowed. "All good. I was hungry. Uh, yeah. We're sending a demo to the Rocktoberfest people down in Black Rock. We're hoping to get in for next year. That would be, like, huge."

"Grindstone just performed there, right?" He sounded certain, but I read the question in his eyes.

"Yeah. My friend sent me the footage—epic. I want to be there next year. I mean, we'd probably be on a smaller stage on the first night...but it's a dream."

"A far way from the Queen Elizabeth Theatre."

The performance venue where I'd played for years.

"Yep. Like, and that's okay. I did what I had to do to make Dad proud when he was alive. I don't regret studying music at the university. I don't wish I'd taken another path. But I also couldn't keep living my father's dream. I had to...basically become my own man."

"Which you seem to have done." He folded the wrapper and dropped it into the recycling bin by his desk. He snagged a water and took a long pull.

"Yeah, I've done all that. For better or for worse. But I've got to get more exposure. Razor Made is just some Canadian Indie rock band. We need more credentials, and followers, to get a spot at Rocktoberfest." *Please understand how important this is to me.*

"And you plan to use your association with my organization to get you that *exposure*?" He used air quotes.

I frowned. "I didn't say that."

"You didn't have to. Our organization has been here for a long time, but suddenly you appear. At the same time, you need to be seen more." He frowned. "It doesn't take a genius to figure out the two things are related."

I wanted to argue.

He was wrong, but I couldn't find the words to refute his assertion. "Wow. You really don't think highly of me." Not what I really wanted to say—but good enough. "I should be going."

"Malik—"

"What?" I hadn't moved from the couch, but I had a plan to leave. I'd wish Bonnie well, grab a few autographed CDs from my SUV, take them—along with the canvas bag—to the café. Then I'd leave this part of town and not return for a while.

Yeah, that was the plan.

Yet, still I sat. Waiting for him to make another pronouncement from on high.

"Life is rarely simple. You want clicks and likes to boost your profile and to get you on the road to a recording contract. Is that about the state of affairs?"

I scratched my chin. "You make it sound like I'm a mercenary—out for all I can get."

"Are you not? You're using us."

"Hey, that's not fair."

"Something can be *not fair* and correct at the same time."

He wasn't wrong.

"How about I compose an anthem? You can decide if it's something you can use. I can make it a full band rock'n'roll, or I can do an acoustic guitar piece. Hell, for you, I'd even play the violin." My playing would be a little rusty after two years of disuse, but I was capable of anything. The instrument would sing in my hands again. I'd find my long-lost love of the violin. For Spencer, I'd do anything.

"That's very generous." He cleared his throat. "And a lot to ask of you."

"Composing and then recording the song is what I do for a living." I gave him a wicked smile. "You know I'm capable."

"I know there are many things you can do. Turns out, I'm slowly discovering them." A frown marred his brow—like he didn't want to admit I had talents beyond getting in trouble.

"Give me a shot—you've got nothing to lose."

He eyed me. "I have plenty to lose. That said, you have something very special that I value—enthusiasm. Even if you're here for all the wrong reasons, you know you want to help. Hell, I don't understand why you're here. The real reason, I mean." He let out a long breath. "Yes, go ahead and write an anthem for us. I can't guarantee we'll use it and I also can't pay you."

My knee-jerk reaction was to challenge him. Not on the pay part—because I knew I was doing this for free. No, I wanted to challenge him on why I was here. Or rather, why he thought I was here. Still, I grinned. "Give me a couple of days."

"Take as long as you like." He rose.

I hesitated. I really didn't want to leave. We'd had fun. Or at least I had. Still, he'd stood and, generally, that meant the other person was supposed to stand as well. For once, I did as I was expected.

Well, that might've been a huge exaggeration. Just, in this moment, I didn't want to let go. Much as I'd felt at my parents' funeral. Of wanting just one second more. To be a better person. To be who they wanted me to be. *Why are you seeking his approval? You know you won't get it, and you damn well don't need it.* I sought the truth in the words my inner voice was providing me but, in that moment, I felt only regret. So I rose and held out my hand. "I'll be in touch."

"Yeah. Great." He grasped my hand.

An arc of electricity passed between the two of us. I felt it.

Judging by the widening of his pupils, he felt it too.

"Jesus, I want to kiss you so badly." Because why not lay everything on the table? If I'd learned one thing from my parents' death, it was that tomorrow was never guaranteed.

Ever.

So, seizing the day held appeal. *Carpe diem* and all that crap.

"This is a bad idea." He whispered the words even as he continued to grip my hand.

"As you like to remind me, I'm not always known for doing the right thing." I tugged. Gently—but insistently.

He stepped into my personal space.

I tipped my head up to maintain eye contact.

He licked his lips.

I grasped his cheeks and pulled him closer.

Our lips touched.

Chapter Eleven

Spencer

I'd spent the last eighteen hours or so trying to convince myself that last night's kiss hadn't been all that I'd made it to be in my mind. That yeah, Malik was a good kisser. But it hadn't meant anything. That we were still just going to go along as acquaintances and that the kiss meant nothing.

To either of us.

Fuck, was I ever wrong.

On all counts.

First, he'd initiated this kiss. That had to mean something. Hell, it meant everything.

Second, his lips were as soft as I remembered.

Third, where last night I'd fought to dominate the kiss, this afternoon I let him lead. He initiated this. He requested this. And, as quickly became evident, he knew what the fuck he was doing. Last night hadn't just been a fluke.

He held my cheeks firmly. He thrust his tongue into my mouth and sought the recesses as he dominated every part of this. He pressed himself against me so I could feel his erection. Denim and khaki were no impediment.

I ran my hands down his flank, along his hips, and down to his ass. I grasped his butt cheeks and thrust against him

He moaned.

Spurred on, I squeezed his pert ass and rutted against him as he continued his assault on my mouth. This was...frenetic, frantic, and hot as fuck.

He pulled back, staring into my eyes with those wide, black pupils. The dark-brown irises were barely visible.

In the back of my mind, I registered the dullness in the room. I hadn't turned on a lamp, and clearly those dark storm clouds had moved in. For once, thank God, my pills were working. I didn't even have a twinge in my head.

"I want to blow you."

My eyes widened, and I shook my head slightly—as if I could jar loose what he was saying. "You want...?"

"To get down on my knees, remove your stiff cock from your jeans, put said cock into my mouth, and blow your mind." He offered a cheeky grin. "I'm pretty sure you're down with that."

I cleared my throat. "I have an employee in the other room."

"Is she going to interrupt?"

"Probably not." I might've squeaked that.

A knock came at the door. "Spencer? They're predicting a heavy rain. You biked, right? You might want to head out."

"Are you going?" Bonnie took the bus, but had a long walk at the end of her trek.

"Well, I was kind of hoping—"

"Go, Bonnie. Try to beat the storm. I'll—" I cleared my throat. "See you tomorrow."

"Great. Thanks, Spence."

I held my breath until the front door slammed. Then I let out that breath. "That was too close for comfort. I never lock my door when I'm in here. Yes, Bonnie knocks. Blossom sometimes just barges in."

He held my gaze. "Are you expecting her today?"

"No. She's at another gig this afternoon. I'm not expecting anyone."

"Should we lock the door? Just to be safe?"

"You still want—"

"To blow you? Hell fucking yes."

I stilled. I'd assumed...well, that he wasn't serious. And that Bonnie's interruption had cooled his ardor.

As if reading my thoughts, he pressed his cock against mine. "You're still interested. I'm still interested."

"The storm..." Because I had to hold on to that last shred of sanity. Of dignity. Of self-control.

"We can throw your bike into the back of my SUV, and I'll drive you home. Or we can just wait out the storm here." He gestured to my couch with his chin. "I can think of lots of ways to make use of that very comfortable couch."

An image of him bending me over the side of said couch and taking me from behind had my cock hardening even further. My breath hitched. "That feels unwise."

He grinned. "As you know, my reputation is for making rash decisions. In truth, I do things deliberately and with contemplation—"

I arched an eyebrow.

"Okay, chaining myself to the bridge hadn't been fully conceived—"

I cleared my throat.

"Fine." He scowled. "I might not have been able to enter the States if I'd been charged."

Finally, I nodded.

"But, other than that, I consider things."

"Last night's council meeting?"

He scratched his lightly stubbled jaw.

Did he shave last night? This morning? How fast does his beard grow? What would that stubble feel like under my fingers?

"You've got the wrong impression of me."

"I've only got what you've given me. Frankly, each of our interactions has shown you to be quick to ideas, laser-focused on execution, and piss-poor at understanding the ramifications of your actions."

He put his hands on his hips. "And who kissed me last night? I'm thinking I'm not the only impetuous one."

"That was—" I pressed my fingers to my kiss-swollen lips. "A mistake."

"And just now?"

"You asked permission. Last night..." I just couldn't continue. Instead, I let the words hang in the air.

"I promise you—like cross my heart and hope to die if I lie—that I welcomed that kiss. I could've said *no*. I could've pushed you off. I could've asked you to back off. You'll note I did none of those things. Instead, I took full advantage. And, given half a chance, I would've dragged you off to a secluded alley and blown you right then. But you ran before I had a chance to say any of that. To do anything about my body's reaction to being near you."

My body's reaction... Was that all this was? Two guys with an itch to scratch? Because, in some ways, we had nothing in common. The age gap, the differences in our education, our passions... On the other hand, we had activism in common. Even if he went about it all wrong, a small part of him must've believed in our cause. We weren't the highest profile. We didn't have the largest budget. Our niche was challenging regulations and bylaws. Zoning issues and respecting treaty rights. Those weren't sexy issues.

And yet he was here.

He stepped toward me and, after clearly telegraphing his movement, he raised his hand to press to my forehead. "What are you thinking? Given your frown, it can't be good. Do you think you can let go of some of that vigilance? Enough so I can bring you pleasure? Because you're wound so tight—"

I lunged toward him and fused our mouths together again.

He saw me. He really saw me. Not just the lawyer trying to run a nonprofit. Not just the guy who always rained on his parade. No, he saw me for who I was. He might not know the extent of my loneliness—but he understood it. Even without words, he communicated his comprehension of my complicated life.

This time, I wrapped my arms around his neck and dragged him closer. I fused our mouths, and when he thrust his tongue into my mouth, I welcomed it. I didn't need to fight for dominance. Last night had been both an expression of desire and, to my shame, anger. Today was all about lust. About getting all I could get. I wanted more...but I didn't know how to ask. My last boyfriend had always figured things out. We'd been...boring. And that had been okay. I'd needed stability. Routine.

Now? Malik Forestal had thrown my orderly world into chaos, and I almost couldn't regret that.

He pulled back and gazed up at me with lust-filled eyes. "You'll let me blow you?"

"Yeah."

"Just so you know—I don't expect reciprocity. Whatever you're comfortable with. This is about putting you at ease."

"I think...maybe if I sit on the couch? I'm worried about your knees."

He snickered. "No worries on that count. Young and strong."

Which, for just half a moment, had me remembering that although I might be strong—in some senses—I wasn't young anymore. Forty wasn't over the hill...but I preferred not to kneel for extended periods of time.

He brushed his cheek against mine. "Whatever makes you most relaxed. I just want your cock inside my mouth as fast as humanly possible."

I cleared my throat. "Yeah, me too." Sort of came out as a croak. "But I have to lock the door. I'll do the outer one—no one has a key except Bonnie. If anyone wants in, they'll have to ring the bell."

"Sounds good." He snagged his glass of water, that sat unattended on my desk, and took a long drink. "Hurry back." He winked.

On that note, I hustled through the front office, locked the front door, and headed back to my office.

The doorbell was loud enough to be heard just about everywhere in the old house, so I didn't worry about closing my office door—that added a layer of privacy.

When I returned, Malik was closing the blinds. "Those clouds are brutal, but no rain yet."

"It's coming."

He met my gaze. "Yeah, it is. Your head?"

"I took my pills."

"Let me know if you need to take more. Let me know if you need me to stop. And, most importantly, let me know what I can do to make you feel good."

"Uh...just about anything?" I had no idea of his level of experience. As a bad-boy rock star, probably a lot. But that was a newer persona. As a violinist with the symphony? Perhaps not as much. *Why are you thinking about his previous partners? For fuck's sake, he'll tell you what he is and is not comfortable doing.* Point well made. I snagged a soft blanket and put it over the rather expensive leather—a relic from Maude's days. The couch, if I continued to treat it well, would last for decades. That said, the thing wasn't nice to bare skin on sticky, humid days.

Malik chuckled. "To contain the mess? Don't worry—I swallow."

I gulped. "I was thinking more of my bare ass on the leather."

"Ah, a man who considers creature comforts—I knew I liked you for some reason."

"The couch was made by a member of a tribe in the interior. Maude sourced everything ethically. I wouldn't make the decision to buy a leather couch today, but the cow would've been slaughtered anyway for food—so this is a way to ensure nothing is wasted." At least that's how I justified it to myself. My sectional at home was faux leather, and that was just fine with me.

"Now is not the time to have a discussion about whether or not you're vegetarian, and—"

"Yes, to both." I grasped the button on my khakis and met his gaze.

"Oh yeah. I'm very much still interested." He palmed his cock—still erect and still contained in the confines of his jeans. "Get comfortable."

I undid the button, lowered the zip, and then let my khakis drop. I sat on the couch and adjusted my hips so my ass was barely on the blanket. Then I palmed my cock.

He hadn't taken his eyes off me the entire time, and he grinned wolfishly. "Oh, this is going to be fun."

My breathing shallowed as he placed himself between my spread thighs and gracefully dropped to his knees. He was still on his knees—as he would have been had I remained standing—but this felt less awkward. Plus, if my knees went a little weak during the orgasm he'd promised, I wasn't going to pitch forward or backward. This just felt...more civilized.

Right up until he nudged my hand away from my shaft. He grasped the base and lowered his head.

The first touch of his tongue against my slit sent more of that electricity shooting through me.

He met my gaze again as he pulled my crown into his mouth.

Chills ran up and down my spine, and desire pooled low in my belly and lower still, in my cock. "Please." Half whisper, half plea.

He winked. Then he drew me into his mouth and down his throat. I worried he might choke, but he clearly knew exactly what he was doing. He sucked hard, hollowing his cheeks, even as he maintained eye contact.

What does he see? My desperation? My desire? My loneliness?

All or perhaps none? Maybe he just saw a guy who really wanted a blow job. It'd been years, and I wasn't going to think about that as he sucked me deeper. As he took my balls in his hands and lightly twisted. Gently squeezed.

Need thrummed through my veins.

Desire ricocheted through my body.

Craving overtook my reasoning.

"I'm coming." I could barely push the words past my tight throat. My entire body was wound so tight, explosion wasn't just possible—it was probable.

He sucked harder.

I came just as hard.

Chapter Twelve

Malik

Having Spencer Fucking Wainright come apart under my ministrations was a sight to behold. One I wouldn't soon forget.

He finally broke eye contact, arched his neck backward, and drew in great lungfuls of air.

I continued to suck until I was certain I'd gotten every last drop of cum. With a satisfied grin, I pulled off him with a little *pop*. Even that didn't bring him down to earth. Although my knees weren't aching, my cock was certainly unhappy at having been neglected for so long. I tried to parse out my options.

"You should—" He gulped. "I should—" He managed to tip his head back so our gazes met.

"I'm good." I offered a broad self-satisfied grin. I hadn't been certain I could actually make him let go of that ever-present vigilance. But he had. In spectacular fashion. I was kind of proud of myself. Oh, who was I kidding? I was fucking blissful.

"But—" Another deep breath.

His color was hectic red. *Should I be worried? He doesn't have a heart condition...right? Just the headaches—* "Are you okay?"

He rolled his eyes.

I took that as a good sign. I pointed to my crotch. "If you can just direct me to a bathroom? I can—"

"Want you. Now. Here."

That took me by surprise. "Uh...okay. Huh. What exactly does that look like?" My intense curiosity wasn't going to be sated until he basically drew me a map.

"I give you a blow job. You fuck me. Way behind that is me giving you a hand job or—"

"I'll take option number two." I grinned. "I mean, you need to come down first, but man, I so want to take your ass." I'd prayed he was a bottom—all the while telling myself he was never going to let me fuck him. No grass was going to grow under my feet. "Sooner rather than later." I pressed the heel of my hand to my crotch.

"Condoms."

I held up a finger with one hand and grabbed my wallet with the other. "Two condoms and two packs of lube. Never leave home without them." I procured them. "I get tested regularly and haven't been with anyone since my last negative test."

"Yeah." He blew out a breath. "I haven't been with anyone since my ex, and I've been tested twice since then."

"Not to get too personal—and you can tell me it's none of my fucking business—"

"He dumped me when I left BioVale."

"Asshole."

He shrugged. "I haven't missed him all that much. What did that say about our relationship?"

"Now's not the time...but I'd love to hear why you left there and came here. I assume the progression was linear...?"

"Yeah. I was on my way out when this job became available. I took that as a sign from the universe that I was doing the right thing. I jumped ship there and came here." His pupils were blown in the low light. "Not a story for today, though."

"That's fair. I'm trying to figure out the best way to fuck you."

He arched an eyebrow, then chuckled. "That doesn't surprise me. Do you mind looking me in the eye?"

My cock stiffened further. "No...I'd prefer that."

"Then missionary style while lying on the couch would work. I've never done it—obviously—but I think it's big enough to hold both of us."

"It's quite long." Certainly longer than most three-seater couches I'd seen.

"Maude was...eclectic. Or eccentric? Now, I can't guarantee she didn't get up to anything—"

"Are you trying to deflate my boner?" I did not want to think of the old lady who used to own this house. I could admire her and not want to know what she'd been up to on that couch.

He chuckled. "All good." He flopped forward and started to untie his shoelaces. He was clumsy, though, and clearly having a tough time.

I knelt before him, gently brushed his hands aside, and undid them myself. I met his gaze.

"Thank you."

"I bet that was hard."

He rolled his eyes. "I don't hate you. I don't have trouble expressing gratitude when someone helps—especially when I know, at some point, I'll be able to return the favor."

"When I'm balls-deep in you, you'll likely remember to thank me."

He barked out a laugh as I removed his shoes. I pulled his pants over his feet and admired the fine blond hair that covered his legs. Slowly, I ran my hands from his large feet, up his muscled calves—I could totally tell he was a cyclist—to his thick thighs. His deflated cock lay in a nest of dark-blond curls. Gently, I stroked it.

"It's not getting up again any time soon—refractory periods are a thing."

"Is that, like, the time between boners?"

"After a climax, yes." He eyed me. "You knew that."

"I might not have been the child prodigy my father wanted, but I am well-versed in all things sex. Especially gay sex. I will say, my mother bought me a couple of books. They might be dog-eared by now."

He arched an eyebrow. "You were having that much sex?"

I grinned. "I'll admit to dating some *nice* boys in university. We always went to their places, and I told my parents I was studying. Since I got straight-As, no one ever questioned it. Well, my mother might've known. My father would've lost his shit. After I joined the symphony, I had fewer hookups. You're going to have to get up so we can reposition the blanket. Unless—"

Valiantly, he pushed off the couch.

I helped him to his feet.

We rearranged the blanket so it covered the entire surface.

I helped him lie back down.

"Living at home was just simplest. I had plans to go out on my own. I was saving diligently because I wanted to buy a condo or something. I didn't want to be a renter and forever caught in that cycle. I'd started looking when—" I winced.

He reached out his hand to run it against my thigh in silent support.

Talk about a boner killer.

I shrugged. "Then it seemed kind of pointless to move. I mean, I live in a beautiful house with an amazing recording studio in the basement. I make enough money to pay the taxes, and I do most of the upkeep myself. It's not in a neighborhood I would've chosen, but it works for me."

"Which neighborhood?"

"Nope. We go down that road and I'm going to lose my enthusiasm completely." I flicked the button of my jeans open.

He spread his thighs.

Now, we were getting somewhere. I'd only planned to ask him to let me write an anthem for this place. Maybe to get a repeat of the kiss. A blow job and now sex hadn't even been on my radar. *Well, maybe a little. When is sex not on your mind?*

Uh...perhaps while singing? Certainly while playing concerts. When I was horsing around with the guys. When Mama Murthi was lecturing—

Holy fuck. You're going to talk yourself out of this gorgeous erection. Pay attention. Ready and willing partner. Go!

Fair enough.

I toed off my cowboy boots—which really didn't go with the rock star persona but I loved them anyway—then shucked my jeans and boxer briefs.

Spencer licked his lips.

I snagged a condom wrapper from the top of his desk where I'd casually tossed it. I opened the packet, removed the condom, then rolled it on. After grabbing the sachet of lube, I made my way over to him. "Are you okay with me prepping you? I know some guys..."

His frantic nods had me trailing off my words into a huge grin. "Yeah, okay." I yanked my shirt over my head and tossed it toward the chair behind the desk.

My nipples puckered in the cold air.

"Those tattoos..." He let out a long breath.

I flexed my arms as I made my way over to him. "You like, eh?" I settled between his thighs on the couch—a tight fit, to be sure, but manageable. I opened the packet of lube and coated my fingers. Then I held his gaze as I ran my fingers around his entrance.

His eyes shone, even in the dim light.

I pressed one finger in.

He nodded.

I added a second. I scissored and twisted and tried to open him up. All the while, we held gazes. Finally, I angled my wrist in just the right way to hit his prostate.

Precum leaked from his tip and he let out a little whimper.

"I've got you, sweetheart. I'll take care of you." Endearments didn't come easy to me. In fact, I almost never used them. With him, though, it felt right. Like he needed the assurance I wasn't some fly-by-night rock star who was going to fuck off to parts unknown after he got laid. That didn't mean I knew how long this relationship was going to last. Just that, for today, I'd take good care of him.

Tomorrow was a whole other thing.

Slowly, I withdrew my fingers.

He whined.

I grinned. I lubed the condom, tossed the wrapper aside, and positioned myself between his thighs. "This might hurt."

He shook his head, even as he gripped his lower lip between his teeth.

Since our gazes still held, and I read no trepidation, I eased myself over him so my cock nudged his entrance.

"Just do it, Malik. Just push in, okay? I can handle it."

Maybe he could...I was an entirely different story. I'd never wanted someone as badly as I wanted him—which made no sense. I barely knew the guy. And what I did know pissed me off. We were opposites in so many ways. We had nothing in common except for a belief we could make the world a better place.

Is that enough?

You're overthinking this. He wants you to fuck him. Why not oblige the guy?

Right.

I pushed in. A tight fit, as I'd expected, but I was committed.

Again, he pulled his lower lip through his teeth.

After another moment, my crown was in. Even as he offered a tentative smile, sweat broke out across my brow. I pushed forward slowly—gauging how much he could take. I'd withdraw a bit, then push forward again. I did this over and over, ensuring he wasn't in pain while fighting off my desire to thrust hard and fast.

That time would come.

When I was fully seated, he wrapped his long legs around my hips.

I cupped his jaw. His pale skin felt even more so next to my dark skin. Such a contrast. Yet I knew in my heart neither of us cared about that. We were all about this moment.

He grinned. "You're going to fuck me now, right? Like you promised?"

"Yeah, like I promised." My grin matched his. I liked that he had a little pillow under his head. A tenderness overwhelmed me as I worried about his comfort.

"Just go for it, Malik. I promise I can take it. I won't break."

I had to believe him.

And so I did.

Chapter Thirteen

Spencer

I don't remember sex ever being this good.

Huh.

Maybe I should focus on that instead of my lackluster sex life to date.

Yeah, that sounds like a good idea.

I didn't break. Far from it. On the heels of a mind-shattering blow-job-induced orgasm, I didn't have huge expectations. Refractory periods were a thing. But one look from Malik and I was hard as a rock. As he fucked me, the need to come again overwhelmed me. Sent me higher and higher as I fought the urge. I didn't want to come before him—that felt rude. That said, I might not have a say in the matter.

He reached between our bodies and grasped my cock. Then he gave it a couple of tugs. "I need you to come." He said the words through gritted teeth. His jerking my shaft met the rhythm of his thrusts as he nailed me. Over and over. Higher and higher.

My skin felt too tight, and electricity arced through me. The sensations overwhelmed and, eventually, holding back became impossible. "I'm going to come." The words were garbled, even to my own ears.

"Thank fuck. Do it, sweetheart. Come for me."

Even as I came—all over his hand, my stomach, and everywhere else—he continued his thrusts. I soared into the air. The oxygen was stolen from my lungs. My vision narrowed even as my rigid body began to relax. I tingled everywhere as I tried to regulate my breathing. Tried to come down from this potent high.

His expression was a mask of concentration. His brow furrowed. Sweat sheened across his forehead. I thought about wiping it off, but then he thrust once more and held himself still. He howled his release as he arched his neck and threw his head back.

I'd never had a lover react so violently. Never had someone push me so hard and high. My own climax had waned—and my cock was finally flaccid—but I still felt energized. Still wanted to stay connected like this forever.

Tires screeched.

Forever? What the hell? One good fuck does not equal forever.

Right. My interior monologue was right. I couldn't possibly be in love. Not with a man who drove me to distraction in all the wrong ways.

He flopped onto me.

I held him tight. He might've been shorter, but he was solid. Muscular. Probably heavier than me. In all the right ways. I cradled his legs between my thighs as I wrapped my arms around him and held him close. He slid from inside me, and that empty feeling hit hard. I shouldn't have been so needy—but I was. I shouldn't want to do this again—but I did.

As his breathing regulated, I grasped the back of his neck and held him close.

"You can touch my hair." His tone was wry.

"I'd never touch without permission." To me, hair was personal. That space that gave us freedom to express who we were.

"I just said you could. I don't know why you'd want to. It's rough."

Experimentally, I touched. And yes, the hair was of a different texture than mine—slightly rougher and way curlier. On impulse, I grasped it and gave a little tug.

A shudder ran through his body. "Fuck, I love that so much. When someone pulls my hair, it makes me hard."

I chuckled. "So soon? Oh, to be that young."

He pressed his nose against me chin. Then he replaced the nuzzling with a light kiss. Finally, he bit. Not hard—but enough to get my attention.

"What did you do that for?"

"You're not old, and even I can't get hard thirty seconds after the best orgasm of my life."

I couldn't dissect his words with clarity.

Okay, he didn't find me old. I did, but we could debate the point later.

He wasn't going to get hard again in the next minute but, more importantly, he'd told me he loved having his hair pulled. Definitely something to keep in mind for another day. *Best orgasm of my life.* How was I supposed to respond? That it had been the same for me? That I didn't ever want to let him go—even though that made no sense?

For the first time, I became aware of the rain lashing against the window. "Well, appears the meteorologist was correct—that sounds like quite a storm."

"You biked, right? I seem to remember..." He trailed off as if thinking rationally was beyond him.

I had sex brain as well. "Yeah. I just live over in Mount Pleasant, so I often bike."

"Downhill on the way to work and uphill on the way home." He said the words dryly.

"Yeah, pretty much. I often wind up showering when I get home—especially if the weather's hot and muggy."

"We're into the end of October."

"That we are."

"What I'm trying to say is we can put your bike in the back of my SUV. I need to drop those CDs off at the café. Then I can drive you home."

"I can take the bus. My bike's safe here overnight."

"Does the bus go from the door here to the door of your house?"

"My condo? Uh, no."

"Then I'll drive you. No sense you getting soaked."

His bossiness was turning me on a little bit, which I found surprising. Especially since I'd come to work here, I'd taken a lot of pride in being responsible for everything. For everyone. Even Blossom—although she didn't feel that way and certainly wouldn't thank me for the idea.

Slowly, he disentangled himself from me and scooted off the couch. "Does this place have a shower? Because I think I stink, and I really don't want to go into the café smelling like spunk."

I burst out laughing. "I agree smelling like sex might be off-putting. Although, frankly, I think you smell good. I like your soap."

He offered a grin. "All natural. I didn't want to wear anything chemical around you."

His words stunned. That he'd put so much effort into preventing me from getting a migraine. "I...uh...thank you."

He dropped a kiss to my cheek. "You're welcome. Now, shower?"

"Yes. Upstairs."

"You joining me?"

I eyed him. "We're just going to shower...right?"

His grin was wicked. "I'd be up for more...but I can behave."

"Well, I appreciate that. Even though we're alone, this is still my workplace. I'd feel awkward—" I gazed at my sweat-slicked spunk-smelling rosy-from-sex body. "Fuck it. If you can get up again, I'll give you a blow job."

He did.

I did.

Then he jerked me off because apparently me giving a blow job had me growing hard as well. Who knew giving pleasure would be so arousing? I hadn't. I'd certainly never been aroused like that when I'd been sucking Paul off.

I resolutely put my ex out of my mind as we loaded my bike into the back of Malik's SUV. Despite our best efforts, we were both soaked by the time we got in. He disregarded my concern over his leather seats and said something about it being his father's *old thing*.

Admittedly, I didn't know a whole lot about SUVs—but I recognized the high-end brand, the fact the vehicle was electric, and I couldn't help but noticing how everything appeared new. Either he rarely used it or he took good care of it.

Despite my best efforts, my breath wound up fogging up the windows while he was in the café. I was *not* going to think about him and Ty. Just because the man was damn attractive, didn't mean he slept with everyone he encountered—men or women. My instinct said bisexual, although that might just have been because I'd spotted him with both genders. Hell, he might even be pan or poly. I didn't have a problem with either—people were free to love whoever they wanted.

He returned, hopped into the SUV, and started the engine with the defrost on high to clear the fog from the windows.

"Sorry."

"No worries." He grabbed a towel from the wheel well behind his seat. He made an attempt to dry his hair. It'd gotten wet during our shower as well.

He caught my gaze. "It's going to be hell later. That's why I just let it go natural with the curls. I'm too lazy to style it and put too much gunk in it."

Experimentally, I touched it.

He arched an eyebrow.

I grasped the hair by the base of his neck and tugged.

He moaned. "Do that again and I'll ask for another blow job right here and now."

I glanced at the windows—now mostly clear. The rain still pelted down. I cocked my head,

"Yeah. Later." He secured his seatbelt, put the SUV in Drive, checked over his shoulder, and entered into traffic. "Will you program the GPS? I should've asked for your address before."

"You were busy."

"Huh?" He executed a smooth right turn.

"With, you know, people." I entered my address into his system.

"Left turn onto Main Street in one kilometer." The computer voice spoke smoothly.

I jolted. "Is that...Irish?"

"Yep. You weren't jealous, were you?"

"Of your sexy sounding GPS? No." I could be obtuse when the situation called for it.

"I meant when I went into the café."

"Why would I be jealous?"

He stopped at a red light and glanced over at me.

Those intense dark-brown eyes held me enthralled.

"Okay, maybe a bit."

He grinned. "No reason to be. Ty is in a very interesting poly relationship with two, uh, interesting people."

"Sounds like a lot of interesting."

He guffawed. "True. I'll admit the unconventionality makes me curious. I'll also say I'm a one-person man. I'm big on monogamy. I demand the same from whomever I'm in a relationship with."

The light turned green and, after looking both ways, he advanced into the intersection. Prudent, given the insanity of Vancouver drivers. And also because he'd lost his parents in a wreck and probably didn't want to go through that.

As a cyclist who frequently had near-misses with drivers, I appreciated his caution. "Monogamy is good."

"Did your ex cheat on you?"

"No." I interlaced my fingers and tightened them.

"Are you lying to me?"

I cast a glance his way, even though his focus was on the road. "No, I'm not lying. I mean, I suppose Paul could've cheated on me. He—" I blew out a breath. "He was very career-focused. I was someone who might help him get ahead. Best I can figure, he wouldn't have risked my ire."

"Would you have been ire-ish?"

"No." Even as I said the word emphatically, I considered. "Well, maybe. I thought we were in a long-term relationship, you know? We talked about marriage sometimes, but we were sort of vague about future plans. Just living for the moment."

"Or so you told yourself."

My breath caught. "Yeah, or so I told myself. It's amazing how easy it can be to lie to ourselves." I scratched my nose.

He executed the left turn onto Main Street. "Who broke it off?"

"He did. When I quit. He wanted a corporate boyfriend who could help him get ahead. I wanted dignity and self-respect. In the end, those two opposing forces were incompatible." I laughed—harsh even to my own ears. "He secured my job for himself—quite a promotion."

"And here you are."

"And here I am." I sniffed. "No regrets."

"You sure?" He stopped at another red light. Traffic was heavy with downtown commuters heading to the suburbs like rats scurrying off a sinking ship. I'd been lucky enough to always live close enough to work so I didn't have to do the commute rat race. That also meant I'd work late without a second thought—what with work being *just around the corner*. In retrospect, in that corporate job, I'd had very little differentiation between the personal and the professional. Which was probably how Paul slotted himself into my life so easily. His ambition was greater than my own, but I admired that. He didn't report to me, so us dating wasn't a big deal. Interesting, though, how he'd suggested we keep it under wraps.

Smart, really.

Because when I took a moral stance on the falsification of data—and had quit—he hadn't been tainted by association. Instead, he'd stayed to *clean up the mess* and to help the company attempt to rehabilitate its reputation.

None of that impressed me.

Good riddance. "Yes, I'm certain it's good riddance. He was a mistake—I just didn't see it at the time. But I do now."

"Well, better late than never, right?"

"Something like that." In Paul's case it would have been better to have never gotten involved with him. Instead to have chosen someone completely outside the corporate realm. Hell, beyond the legal profession would've been an even better choice.

Except, if I'd done any of that, then I would likely not be sitting in this SUV, on this particular day, with this amazing man.

Yes, grudgingly I was willing to admit I might've been off base in my assumptions about him.

A little bit, anyway.

He still had a way to go before I was willing to admit he was a true believer. "Do you have rehearsal tonight?"

With only the slightest hesitation at the amber light, he ensured oncoming traffic was stopped, and he eased us onto East 2nd and began the slow ascent. He'd cut across Brunswick, shimmy across East 5th, and then take St. Georges Street to East 6th. We'd be at my place in no time at all.

Now or never. "Do you want to come up?"

"Huh?" He executed the next turn smoothly.

I cleared my throat. "Would you like to come up? I mean, it's not great or anything—"

"Way to temper a guy's expectations." He made the next turn.

"And I have a stubborn cat. If you're, like, allergic or something."

"I'm not." He turned onto my street.

"In one hundred meters, your destination will be on your left."

I let out a long breath. "I'm asking you to come up if you're interested. If you're not, then I'm happy to thank you for the ride, grab my bike, and head inside."

The rain had lessened a bit.

A very little bit.

"What's your cat's name?"

"Huh?" I rubbed my forehead. "Oh... Moses."

He chuckled. "I bet there's a story behind that name."

"There is."

"Then I accept. I can meet Moses and hear the story behind his name." He offered me a wicked grin.

"I'll give you the code for the parking garage."

Chapter Fourteen

Malik

Spencer's condo was...cozy.

Somehow, I pictured him in something more upscale. Not a fifty-year-old building. He assured me that the roof had recently been replaced and his unit's soundproofing had been increased when it had been renovated just before he bought it. And that the place cost him more than comparable units, but with the upgrades done during the reno, the investment was worth it.

In fact, he rambled like a nervous teenager as he gave me a tour of the kitchen, living room, bathroom, and the micro room he called the bedroom. The open Murphy bed was literally the only thing in the room except a nightstand.

Moses lay in the middle of Spencer's navy-blue comforter, shedding his orange hair. The tabby gave me a long look, blinked, then jumped off the bed with a decidedly impatient *meow* as he headed to the kitchen.

Obediently, Spencer followed. "I know it's dinnertime. I'm sorry I'm late."

Slowly, I followed. "You're usually home before dinnertime?"

He glanced at me as he opened a tin of wet cat food that, admittedly, smelled pretty gross.

"What? Oh no. This is about the time I always get home."

"So why are you apologizing to him? He doesn't appear horribly hard done by. A little scrawny, but I'm going to assume that's not because—"

"Oh no." Spencer dished out the food onto a nice plate and put it on the floor.

Moses attacked it as if he hadn't eaten in a million years.

I arched an eyebrow.

Spencer met my gaze. "He just, like, almost died as a kitten. He's always been...scrappy." He scratched his cheek. The light stubble under his nails made my fingers itch—I wanted to be the one scratching him. "I give him plenty of food, but he never seems to gain weight. His vet says not to worry, so I try not to." Even as he said the words, his hand fluttered against his chest.

Slowly, I advanced toward him.

He didn't retreat.

I grasped his hand and used it to lever him toward me. "I'm not judging you by the size of your cat." I gripped his hip.

Then replayed my words in my mind.

"That came out wrong."

He laughed. Perhaps a little more forced than natural, but I'd take it for a win.

"Sweetheart, why are you so nervous?"

His gaze shot to mine—those luminous-green eyes sparkling in the bright lights of the kitchen. "Sweetheart?"

I shrugged. "You don't like it? I'm certain I can come up with something else."

Slowly, he shook his head. "I like it." This time, the laugh was genuine. "I shouldn't...but I do."

"Because it shows a level of intimacy you wouldn't ascribe to us?"

"Frankly?"

I nodded.

"Yes."

"Spencer, not two hours ago, my cock was up your ass. I don't know how more intimate two people can be."

His eyes widened. Whether at some realization or just because of my crudeness, I couldn't be certain.

"I'm not good at this, Malik. In retrospect, things in my last relationship were...sterile."

I wrinkled my nose. "Gross."

Another laugh. "I've been in other relationships over the years. I'm not a forty-year-old virgin."

"May I say I'm relieved at that? If you had been, I would've done things very differently."

"You been with many virgins?" His tone took on a teasing quality.

"Uh..." I gaze up at the ceiling as if in contemplation. In truth, I knew the answer. "Nope. Not my jam. I want a guy who's as experienced as I am. I don't want to be worrying about—" I winced. "That sounds wrong. I mean, I always care about my partner's pleasure. I want him to come first. Well, whenever possible."

"I think I get the picture."

"With you—" I scratched my eyebrow.

"You didn't have to go easy on me."

"Right. I mean, I totally would have. But you made it clear you were okay with—" I winced.

He chuckled. "Drilling me into the couch. Totally appreciated. Which reminds me that I have to launder that blanket and take it back in the morning." He'd tucked it into a garbage bag and brought it home.

"It'll be a challenge to cycle to work tomorrow with that."

"I can cram it into a large duffel bag and haul it over my shoulder." He peered to his sliding glass door that exited to a small balcony. "Or I might just drive. I'll see what the forecast for tomorrow is."

"If you decide to cycle, I can drop you and your bike off."

He frowned.

I waited.

His mouth opened. Then shut. Then opened again. "Did you just invite yourself to spend the evening?"

"Do you have lube and condoms?" I nuzzled behind his ear. "Are you up to more?" He hadn't taken any more pills. *Should I worry? Should I bring it up? Does he take care of himself or does he need a keeper?*

Are you offering yourself?

That question—from the inner recesses of my mind—caught me off guard. Yeah, I'd called him sweetheart. I'd driven him home. I was worried about him.

But those things didn't constitute being in a relationship.

Did they?

I didn't have a good answer for that.

"Dinner first. If you're still here after I've fed you, then I'm open to offers." He rubbed his cheek against mine.

I pulled back, eyeing him. "Should I be worried?"

"I'm a vegetarian. So unless you're planning to order in—"

"I can buy dinner."

"You bought lunch. I'm happy to cook."

"Sounds great." I perched on a bar stool on one end of the galley kitchen as he fried up a couple of veggie burgers on an indoor grill.

As we sat and ate them—along with baby carrots in butter, cauliflower with cheese sauce, and French bread—I grinned. "I think these would be even better on the grill."

His returning grin was just as quick. "They are. I have one that I use a few times a year. I'm not thrilled about using gas, but there's nothing quite like charbroiled."

"You'll have to prove that to me." I pointed to the burger. "That's better than I expected."

"Of all the veggie burgers out there, these are my favorites." He offered one of his shyer smiles.

"I'll bet you've tried them all."

"Yep. When new ones come out, I try them as well. And always come home."

"Were you always a vegetarian?"

He scrunched his nose. "That's complicated."

"One's relationship with food often is." I dipped some cauliflower into the delicious cheese sauce. "You don't have to share."

"It's my parents."

I stilled. *Is he going to ask for reciprocity? Is he going to want me to talk about my relationship with my parents? With my father? Talk about complicated—*

"I was born in the mid-1980s."

"Okay." I grinned. "That makes you *way* older than me." I made certain to emphasize the *way*. In truth, there were about a dozen years between us, and I couldn't have cared less.

He arched an eyebrow.

I popped the cauliflower into my mouth.

He sighed. "My parents were on the leading end of the environmentalism movement. For them, it started with *no nukes* and ended with *fossil fuels are evil*."

I swallowed. "No nukes?"

"Yeah. They protested again nuclear proliferation. They were convinced the world was going to end in a mushroom cloud. They even attended the *Refuse the Cruise* protest in Vancouver back in '83. Before I was born, but they've regaled me with stories since I was a toddler. I mean, Vancouver declared itself a nuclear-weapon-free zone. Like with Americans in Alaska to our north and Washingtonians to our south didn't somehow factor into things. No one was going to bomb Vancouver. As far as they're concerned, their protests brought an end to nuclear proliferation."

I squinted. "Did they?"

"Don't say nuclear in their presence. With all the shit going on in the world today, they're convinced it's only a matter of time. They're prepared to get out their outfits from the eighties and go out and protest again."

"Okay." I scratched my jaw. "So the no nukes was also environmentalism?"

He blinked at me. "Nuclear is horrific for the environment."

"Right. I knew that." *Say something intelligent.* "I thought British Columbia is primarily hydro-powered."

"We are."

"Do we have nuclear power plants?"

"We do not."

The way he said that made me think I should've known this. "Just pipelines."

His expression darkened as he furrowed his brow. "Yes. The oil's not ours. But the oil people have to get it to market in Asia, so they build pipelines across our pristine wilderness."

Back on solid footing. "Often without consulting with Indigenous tribes."

"And offering them paltry amounts as compensation. It's…" He flapped his hand.

"Frustrating?"

"Yes." He speared a baby carrot. It slid in the butter, skipped off his plate, and landed on the table.

I grabbed it and popped it into my mouth.

As I hoped, that made him smile. "My parents raised me to be respectful of Indigenous peoples, Mother Nature, and the creator of all things."

"God?"

He shook his head. "No. Virulently anti-religion." He squinted. "The creator of all things is sort of like Mother Nature, only more powerful. Anyway, humans are supposed to be caretakers of the earth, but we're destroying it. If my parents could, they'd live in a shack off the grid and survive on berries."

"And yet something tells me they don't."

"Nope." He again attempted to spear a carrot and this time, succeeded. "My mother's parents were loaded."

"Your grandparents."

"Yep."

That confused me—why not just refer to them as his grandparents?

"I never met them."

"Oh." An answer to my unasked question.

"Huge estrangement. My grandfather was big into oil, and my mother was a radical environmentalist—the two didn't go together.

Like, oil and water." He snickered. "Anyway, I lived with my parents in a tiny one-bedroom apartment, and they worked for nonprofits. Making a difference."

"Like you." I was still struggling to hold on to the narrative because clearly I was missing something—I just couldn't figure out what it was.

He gazed around his condo. "I live in the lap of luxury compared to the way I lived as a kid. Then one day, everything changed."

"In what way?"

"My grandfather died. Naturally, he left his estate to his widow."

"Your grandmother."

"Yep. And she passed the next year."

"I'm sorry." Wholly inadequate, but something needed to be said.

"I'm not. I mean, it's sad they died, but everyone dies." His laugh sounded hollow. "My grandmother had never updated her will. She left most of her estate to my mother with a small amount set aside for any potential grandchildren."

"You."

"Me."

"What did that mean?"

"I thought it might mean we could move into a bigger apartment. Heck, I thought maybe we could move into my grandparents' house. I'd never been in anywhere so grand."

"No?"

"Nope. We only went once—to settle my grandparents' estate. The house was put on the market, and my parents donated all the money."

"That doesn't sound..." His look had me stopping.

He waved me off. "It sounded good, but I was tired of sleeping on a pull-out couch. Most of my friends had bedrooms of their own. I understood my parents eschewing wealth...but a bed of my own? I was a teenager by then and fed up with all of it. When I turned eighteen,

I took my education fund and headed to the University of British Columbia. I entered the business school and bided my time until I could go to law school."

I broke off a small piece of bread. "So basically everything your parents didn't believe in."

He offered a wicked grin. "Exactly. I mean, don't get me wrong, I believed in many of their causes. I just didn't believe one had to live in penury to make a difference."

The starkness of our circumstances struck me. He lived in a fifty-year-old one-bedroom condo in Mount Pleasant while I lived in a mansion in Arbutus Ridge. Shame hit hard and fast.

Something must've shown on my expression, because he quickly shook his head. "I'm not saying that. Hell, I lived in a nice downtown condo—all steel and glass and expensive. I still contributed to charities, but I focused on a job that I thought would make a difference. Don't you see?"

Slowly, I shook my head.

He nodded, as if understanding my confusion. "I worked with a leading-edge biomedical research company. Their innovations were making a difference in people's lives, and they did plenty of charity work. Well, maybe charity's not the right word. But they'd extend treatment beyond what was required for the trials. They seemed to care about their patients."

Something in his tone caught my attention. "But something changed?"

"Yeah. We had this really big project. I can't talk about it because my severance came with an NDA. I think nondisclosure agreements are bullshit—and I didn't care about the money—but they threatened to report me to the bar association of British Columbia for breach of trust. Which—" His face made this weird expression that I read as *I sort of did.* "The money didn't mean anything. I donated it all. But then I couldn't make the mortgage payments on my condo in the sky. I had enough equity that, when I sold the place, I was able to buy this one. No floor-to-ceiling windows. No view except the trees behind the building. Hell, I face north, so I never get direct sunlight."

Whereas I live in a mansion with massive windows on all sides. The floor-to-ceiling is two stories in the kitchen and family room. I could fit thirty people in that space without anyone feeling cramped. The dining room sat twenty. Occasionally I talked my bandmates and their families into joining me. Inevitably, we ignored the dining room and opted for the family room, kitchen table, and bar stools at the island counter. Casual. Comfortable. "This is still a really nice place. You might not get sunlight, but your recessed lighting is bright. I mean, it's dark and dreary outside, but you've got a cozy place here."

He chuckled. "Cozy, it is. I just realized—I've never asked you where you live. Or, perhaps more succinctly...you've never told me."

I panicked.

Chapter Fifteen

Spencer

I f not for Malik's dark complexion, I would've said all the color drained from his face. He definitely took on a stillness that I didn't associate with him. Yes, we'd sat down and shared two meals today. Both times, though, he'd appeared restless. Almost like a caged tiger, ready to bolt when the cage door opened. I didn't like to think of him as caged, or even restrained. *He's probably doing it for you. So you don't freak out and accuse him of not thinking things through. Of not being aware of consequences.* Still, he remained motionless. "I mean, you don't have to tell me. No big deal. Here I am, running off at the mouth. You might be living in someone's basement, or couch surfing, or—I don't know—living in your SUV." Although I probably would've noticed. "Truly, it's none of my—"

"I live in a seven-bedroom, six bathroom, five-thou-sand-square-foot mansion on extensive grounds in Arbutus Ridge. Worth eight figures, no less." He rubbed his forehead. "My bandmates know where it is because there's a recording studio in the basement.

My parents' life insurance paid off the house, and gives me an annuity to pay the taxes on the place every year. For spending money—like to feed myself and keep the lights on—I have to work. Which was, undoubtedly, my father's plan. He thought I'd stay with the orchestra until I retired. Ha. More fool him. I should just sell the place—" He rubbed his face. "But my mother loved it. She decorated it to her tastes." His voice caught. "As long as I leave it as it is, then a part of her still lives on. I never go into the primary bedroom. I never enter her library or my father's den. Those places are—" He placed his hands over his face.

Unbidden, I moved to crouch before him. "Sacred spaces. I get it. I really do. It's not the same, but I feel that way in This Land is Ours's offices. Like Maude built this place and I have a legacy to maintain it. I know it's not the same—"

He pulled his hands away from his face and wiped at the tears. "It is the same. I get it. I live in a shrine and I don't have the courage to change it. Hell, I don't know if I want to. I've never lived anywhere else. Until I quit the orchestra, I'd never considered doing anything else. Somewhere along the way, I rebelled against my dad. But only after he was gone. And not in a malicious way. I mean...he was a tyrant. Always knew what was best. Insisted on being right all the time. I was terrified by and respected him at the same time."

"But you wanted something different."

"Yeah. The orchestra was great...but I needed a way to express myself, and that wasn't the right venue."

"And Razor Made is." I ensured the words came out as a statement—not a question. He loved his band. That came through in the music, the videos, and the way he smiled when he mentioned them.

He cocked his head. "You get it." Gently, he stroked his index finger down my cheek. "Sorry to get all weepy."

I cupped his cheek. "You're entitled. It's only been a few years—since you lost them and since you quit a safe and secure life and moved into something...less stable."

"Yeah. I mean, I could rent out my recording studio for tons of money... But I don't want people to know where I live. What my worth is."

"Money's nice, for certain." *Especially when you have little.* Still, I pressed my hand over his heart. "This is what counts. What's inside you. What you do to express that."

"I'm not a fly-by-night."

I cocked my head.

"You think I'm a flash in the pan. Here today, gone tomorrow. I believe in what you're doing—that Indigenous rights and the environment are so tied together that they can't be separated. That if we help ensure our Indigenous brothers and sisters are protected—especially their land—then we can rest a little easier since they're better stewards of the land than anyone else could be."

He was probably right. Aside from a few die-hard environmentalists, most tribes cared for the land in a way I, as a white person, was only beginning to understand. My work was just one piece in a massive puzzle. But if I could do some good, then all was not lost. "I'm coming to understand that you're more than just a guy who wants clicks and likes."

With a weak smile, he replied, "High praise—coming from you."

Then he grasped my hands and urged me up. Instead of letting me retake my seat, though, he sort of tugged me onto his lap.

"I'm too heavy." I had to protest this position—even as I encountered the intimacy of it. I'd never sat in someone's lap before. The feeling was...extraordinary. Like someone wrapping me in a warm blanket. I wound my arms around his neck and nuzzled my nose into his shoulder as he held me. I might've been taller, but he was more muscular. Stronger.

Perhaps better able to face the world—despite his belief of a weakness. But where he saw a fault, I saw only strength. He'd endured the unimaginable and had come out the other side. Hell, he was a rock star. Perhaps only known in Vancouver indie circles for the moment...but he was going places. He had talent and a band who clearly adored him.

"Uh...can I ask a question?"

I pulled back from the embrace to gaze at his stunning dark-brown eyes. "Sure. You can ask me anything." I envisioned some dark, deep secret. Something I'd never shared with anyone. I had a few of those.

"Well, since you offered—" He grinned. "I want to ask about that ex-asshole of yours. But first—" He gestured with his chin. "Is your cat allowed on the table?"

I turned and, to my horror, found Moses licking the butter off my uneaten carrots. "Moses." Part exasperation, part annoyance, part pride. Mostly annoyance.

He kept right on licking.

Malik chuckled. "I think it's cute."

"You just didn't want to finish your vegetables."

His expression turned horrified. "He'd better not aim for my cheese sauce. It'll be a duel to the death."

I laughed. And, a little shakily, I slid off his lap.

Moses, possibly sensing the moment was over, leapt down from the table. I picked up my plate, moved to the kitchen, and dumped everything into the organic compost. "Well, that was interesting."

"Mmm." Malik appeared with his empty plate—and his mouth full of food.

I grinned. "Good, eh?"

He nodded vigorously as he put the plate on the counter.

"Are you, uh..." I let out a long breath.

He swallowed. "Are you asking me to? Do you want me to?"

I stepped into his personal space. "I'm asking. I want."

He grinned. "Then I'm all yours. Do you need to take any meds?"

His question was as casual as anything. That he was thinking about my health—without being overbearing—meant everything. "I'm okay."

"Cool. Now, do you have a spare toothbrush?"

"In a container in the drawer under the bathroom sink." I was vaguely amused dental hygiene was a top priority.

"And lube? Condoms?"

"Small box of condoms—not expired. Big container of lube." Because I was single—and still horny. I wasn't going to mention that I'd been jerking off to images of him the past couple of nights.

"I like your priorities. And the cat?"

I eyed Moses who sat on my barstool, indolently licking his paw. "He can take the couch tonight. I'm not sharing my bed with you *and* him."

Malik glanced over his shoulder. "Does he know that?"

"Uh." I bit my lower lip. "It might be that we've shared a bed every night since I brought him home." To Malik's raised eyebrow, I added, "Yes, I haven't had sex since just before I rescued him. The ex I'd rather not talk about."

He wrapped his arms around my waist and pulled me tight. "Okay. You go first—I'll clean up and have a heart-to-heart with Moses."

Uncertain what that meant, but with my heart rate kicking up, I headed to the bathroom. After brushing my teeth and stripping, I headed into the bedroom. I tossed my clothes in the hamper, then pulled back the top sheet and duvet. I had no idea what to expect, but my imagination was working overtime. Should I be preparing myself?

Were we going to have sex? What if he wanted to bottom? I was fine with that...although topping wasn't always my happy place. With him, though, I'd gleefully make an exception.

The sound of the toilet flushing had me hustling into bed.

I was retrieving the lube and a couple of condoms from my nightstand when he strode in—buck naked. Which was impressive given the small size of my condo.

He grinned wickedly. "I think we're going to have fun tonight."

"Yeah, me too."

And we did.

Chapter Sixteen

Malik

Creed nudged me with his foot against my shin.

I met his gaze.

He grinned wickedly. "Okay, you've got to be thinking about someone. A gal? A dude? An enby? Just something, because you keep getting this look on your face—the look you get when you're all smitten."

I scowled. "Smitten?"

He shrugged. "Well, it doesn't happen often...but it has happened. You've met someone."

We were taking a break from rehearsing, standing near the wet bar in the basement next to the recording studio. Reese was in the bathroom, and Freddie was still at the keyboards—trying to work out a melody in his head that only he could sort out.

"Do you think he's composing something new?"

Creed shrugged. "Anything's possible. He might be tweaking Reese's composition on that last song. I think he's adding to it."

I scratched my chin. "I thought the song was good."

"So did I...but he might be able to make it better. It'll be up to Reese if she accepts the changes or not."

"What changes?" The composer of said song—and our bassist extraordinaire—pushed me aside as she made her way over to the bar fridge. She opened it and grinned. "Thanks for stocking up."

"On blue energy drinks?" I wrinkled my nose. "Only one, okay? We don't need you rocketing into outer space." I couldn't fathom how much caffeine was in those things.

Even as I had the thought, my electric tea kettle whistled that the water was boiling.

Reese moved out of my way so I could set my Earl Grey to steep—something else I got from my mother. I'd add lemon if we were doing a lot of singing. Today was more jamming with the music than worrying about lyrics.

As my tea steeped, Freddie sauntered over.

I opened the fridge, pulled out a can of root beer, and handed it to him.

He grinned, cracked the top, and downed half of it.

Then belched.

Yep, that was Freddie.

"And you wonder why you can't get a girlfriend." I tossed my tea bag into a compost container, added half a teaspoon of brown sugar, and stirred.

"What I really want to know is who Malik's dicking." Creed raised his ice water with a slice of lime in salute.

I glared.

Reese laughed. "You know, I've been asking myself the same question. I'm wondering if it's that guy from the television."

I blew on my tea to cool it down. "What guy?"

"You remember that interview?" She waggled her eyebrows.

"He's married and way too old." The anchor was super adorable—if one was into silver foxes. Me? Blond guys with soft-green eyes—

Creed elbowed me. "You know she's talking about that do-gooder. What was his name?" He snapped his fingers several times. "Oh, I remember. Spencer." He drew the name out, emphasizing each syllable.

Heat raced to my cheeks. I prayed my dark skin would prevent my best friend from seeing how close to the mark he was.

Okay, bullseye. Dead center.

"I don't know what you're talking about."

"Do you not?" Reese grinned. "Then what are the new lyrics in your notebook?"

"Hey!" I rolled my eyes. "Is there no such thing as privacy around here?"

My three bandmates burst out laughing.

"Uh, absolutely not." Creed eyed Reese. "What kind of lyrics?"

I continued to glare.

She shrugged. "I was checking something out for our last song—the one Freddie's not happy with."

"Hey!" He glared.

"Just calling it as it is. We'll get it sorted. We have time." She sipped her energy drink. Then she pivoted her attention to me. "What lyrics? What melody? What are we working on now?"

"I just..." I scratched my chin. "Like..." I floundered.

Creed nudged my shin again.

"Yes, I'm sort of seeing that guy from the television. From the nonprofit. Yes, I'm writing an anthem for his organization that none of you are obliged to be part of. Yes, I'm trying to work out the lyrics, the melody, and the visuals in my head all at the same time." Finally, after pushing all that out, I took a breath.

My best friend chuckled. "I knew you were dicking with someone."

I rolled my eyes.

Freddie raised his hand. "Visuals?"

I nodded. "Like, cinematographically. The images. Whether we're just doing a video or if, during our concert, we project something."

"You mean like the holograph that Blade does?" He cocked his head, apparently intrigued.

Blade and Hellsbane made their first appearance at Rocktoberfest a few years ago and had broken onto the scene with a splash and their holograph of Blade singing.

"Well, I hadn't been thinking of that. More of projections on a screen behind us. Like they're from an old projector. I'd need to go culling archival footage—and gets lots of permissions—but I can see something like that, right? Against a screen?"

"Some venues might have a back wall we can use. Otherwise, we'd have to rent a screen." Reese rubbed her fingers together, miming money. Like how much this was going to cost.

From the moment I quit the orchestra, I'd been very conscious of how much I spent. Maintaining a house this big took a lot of money—property taxes, repairs, electricity, gas, and other shit. Some of which I hadn't had a clue about. My father's lawyer had figured out most things for me and I could consult her when I needed to. For an astronomical fee. So I preferred to watch my bank balance carefully and not splurge. I might be twenty-seven with poor impulse control—sometimes—but I wasn't ever going to risk losing this place. "We might be able to partner with a company. In the film industry? Give them a sponsorship or something? Use their logo in our promos?"

Freddie snickered. "You think some big film people are going to lend us equipment?"

"They will if we get to Rocktoberfest." I took a drink of my tea. "I have plans."

"You have dreams." Freddie downed the rest of his root beer and belched again. "Nothing wrong with aspirations."

"Let me ask Mama if she knows anyone." Creed gestured toward our equipment. "We should get started again. I want to get home before midnight."

"Going to turn into a pumpkin?" Reese with the gentle teasing.

"You know Mama Bear likes to have all her cubs tucked in before the witching hour." I winked at Creed. Personally, I loved that Mama took such good care of her kids. Perhaps too much, though. My friend really needed to move out and get a life of his own. Often I'd considered inviting him to move in, but that felt wrong. Not so much that my parents wouldn't have approved—although they wouldn't have—but that if I brought someone here, someone to share the space with me, they would have to be pretty damn special. I loved Creed, but I didn't feel *that* way about him. Even in a home as cavernous as this one, I worried about stepping on his toes. Or, more likely, him stepping on mine.

"Woof. Woof." Freddie grinned.

We all turned to him with varying looks of confusion.

"What? That's a bear."

Creed bust out laughing. "Dogs woof. I have no idea what a bear sounds like, but that isn't it."

"Wait." Freddie frowned. "If you don't know what a bear sounds like, how do you know it doesn't sound like a dog?"

My mind screeched. Really, neither of them was talking sense. Which was completely par for the course.

"Show me what you've got." Reese pointed to my notebook. "We can worry about projections after we've got a melody and lyrics."

Ever the practical one. I might be the front man for this band, but Reese was the common sense and the brains. Too bad she couldn't write lyrics worth shit.

Four hours later as I lay in bed, after my bandmates had gone home, I tried to recreate Spencer's condo in my mind. About five hundred square feet? Give or take? Plus that pint-sized balcony.

Huh.

The primary bedroom, bathroom, and walk-in closet in this house were almost that size.

Give or take.

So his entire life could fit into my parents' bedroom.

That thought sobered.

Last night, as he'd drifted in and out of consciousness—well, a sort of sex-drunk haze—he'd talked about his old condo in the sky. The boyfriend he'd believed himself in love with until when, after Spencer had done the moral thing, the asshole Paul had stepped up to take over in a rather immoral fashion.

Instantly, I hated the guy. Sounded like a pompous jerk.

Spencer deserves so much better.

Yeah, but did that mean me? I was disorganized, scatterbrained, hyperfocused on music, and wanting to make a difference in the world.

While also being obsessed with likes and clicks.

Blossom loved that about me.

Spencer detested it.

With good reason. He saw me as a flash in the pan. As someone not serious.

So you'll just have to prove that he's wrong.

Easy, right? Show him my brilliance with the song and—

What? He's going to fall at your feet in gratitude? Invite you to move into his micro-condo? Make room in his bed for you?

That was a legitimate question because, when Spencer'd crept out to go to the bathroom in the middle of the night, Moses had clearly decided he'd had enough of being ignored. Somehow, three of us had fit on that queen-sized bed.

Darn cat.

Super cute. Tragic backstory. Pain in the ass.

What if you invited him to move in here?

My mind rebelled. Not so much at the idea of being with Spencer all that time—no, I didn't mind that at all. I just couldn't figure out how his cat would cope. Would he be lost all the time? Would he be able to find the litter box? Would he scratch my mother's draperies?

Would you care?

Ridiculous. One day and night of amazing sex was *not* enough to base a relationship on. Hell, before I went to his office yesterday, he'd still been mad at me. For the city-hall thing. For the Lion's Gate Bridge thing.

I have to get back into his good graces.

Or was I there already? Did a good fucking wipe away all the bad shit I'd done? I just didn't know.

We'd exchanged hand jobs in the shower this morning. Since the rain was still coming down, he'd opted to drive his electric car to work, and I'd driven myself home. I'd spent most of the day trying to work out a song in my mind, and then we'd had rehearsal.

You can't show him the song until it's perfect.

No, I couldn't. So I'd have to work harder to make everything the very best that I could. Perhaps by the time I finished, I might know where I stood with him.

Before I could do something as shmoopy as shooting off a text to him telling him that I missed him, I powered down my phone and went to sleep.

Chapter Seventeen

Spencer

*J*ust because he hasn't called in four days, doesn't mean it's over and you'll never hear from him again. Because, honestly, have you called him? Thanked him for fucking you repeatedly and being willing to share a small bed with both you and your damn cat?

Short answer?

No.

Saturday morning, I sat in my office and stewed. Today was the end of the month, and I had a last few things to resolve before I sent all the paperwork off to our accountant. The task could've waited until Monday, but I didn't have anything else to do. Didn't have anywhere else to be.

Moses certainly wasn't going to miss me.

Malik had been radio silent.

I hadn't contacted him, though. So that niggled.

My cell phone buzzed with an incoming text.

Malik.

We'd exchanged numbers, and I tried to tamp down my excitement at seeing his name. I tapped on the message.

—*What if we rent a plane with a message at the back shaming politicians who support Big Oil?* —

What the hell? —*No. Too expensive. Naming and shaming don't always work.* —

I waited.

—*What if we do a sit-in protest at the provincial legislature?* —

—*No. And get arrested? Just no.* —

—*What if we picket Member of Parliament's constituency offices?* —

I bit my lip. —*No. Not very effective as they're never there and we'd irritate the staff.* —

—*Are you a stick-in-the-mud?* —

—*No. My floor is pristine. There is no mud.* —

—*Are you mad at me?* —

That comment gave me pause. When he'd been inside me? No. Right now? Sort of. —*Yes.* —

A long silence.

My phone buzzed with an incoming call.

Malik.

Again, my heart rate kicked up. I swiped and casually said, "Hello?"

"You're such a spoilsport."

"Well, I wouldn't go that far. I'm practical and—"

"What are you doing?"

I blinked. "What?"

"Right now. What are you doing?"

"I'm finishing off month-end paperwork for our accountant. Then I'm working on my presentation to my local Member of Parliament. She says she's pro-environmentalism. I want to take her at her word, but I also think it's important for her to know what her constituents think. I have a petition—"

"And you think that blasting a presentation to your MP is going to stop them?"

I wasn't certain I liked his tone of disbelief. "Yes. Now go away."

"Where are you?"

I sighed. "At my office. Where else would I be?"

"The nice house in Strathcona?"

"Well...yes. You were here on Tuesday." *When you fucked me on the sofa I'm seriously thinking about replacing because of all the memories.*

He chuckled. "Yeah, I remember. So you're there now?"

"I'm no longer standing behind that statement because I don't like your tone." Teasing? Lascivious? Promising a repeat? Making fun of me? I just couldn't be certain. Then I noticed the silence was far too long. "Malik? Malik? Malik?" Each time I said his voice, I injected urgency—because that reflected my growing panic. "Shit. What are you doing? I can feel in my bones that you're about to do something stupid." I drew air into my lungs. "Answer me."

Another chuckle. "I'm out front. Can you come here? I need to show you something."

I eyed my paperwork, decided Monday morning was just fine, swept it into a folder to put in my desk, locked the desk, locked the laptop in the safe, and then hotfooted it out of the office. I set the alarm, closed and locked the front door, then headed down the walkway to Malik.

Who leaned against his SUV as if he didn't have a care in the world. His clear nonchalance caught me off guard. "What do you want?"

"Can you get into the car? I need to show you something. Just around the corner. It'll take, like, two minutes."

With some trepidation—as well as intense curiosity—I got into his SUV.

He shut my door, winked, then rounded the hood and hopped in his side. After securing his seatbelt, we took off.

And four minutes later, arrived at MacLean Park.

The streets were lined with vehicles, but someone was pulling out just as Malik drove up.

"You must have a horseshoe up your ass. I never find a parking space that easily when things are busy." Brushing aside my pique, I said, "What's going on? Why are things so busy?"

He backed into the parking space with practiced ease, put the SUV in Park, cut the engine, and grinned. "Just a day at the park." He exited his vehicle.

I did the same. The sound of music filtered through as I gazed over to the park and got my first good look. I noted about twenty-five motorcycles along Heatley Avenue. Then we headed into the park. The splash pad was closed, obviously, what with it being the first of November. But the rest of the area was filled with food tents and people milling about—mainly kids and families. Well, and a bunch of burly men and interesting women clad in leather. Safe to assume at least some of them were bikers. "Uh, what's going on?" I looked for a sign but didn't see one.

"This is a fundraiser. For Movember. You know, for prostate cancer."

I'd heard of Movember, of course. When men grew their mustaches to raise money for prostate cancer. My problem was my mustache always came in patchy and I looked like I had a mouse pelt over my lip. To save everyone from staring at me and pitying me, I just made a donation and kept shaving.

"So why are we here?"

Malik grabbed my hand as if this was the most natural thing in the world to do. "We're going to eat hot dogs and cotton candy and drink too much soda. We're going to smile at the families, and we're going to listen to the great indie band who are playing. In other words—we're going to have fun."

I had my doubts. But Malik had chosen to invite me...so how was I to turn this opportunity down?

He guided me to the first vendor, where we bought hot dogs and colas. I was able to get a veggie dog, so I was grateful. As adamant as I was about being vegetarian, sometimes that rigidity put me in a tight spot. Sometimes I chose to be polite over stubborn. Rarely. Today, if I'd only had a meat option, I might've made an exception. That was how much I liked Malik.

Wait. I thought he irritated the shit out of you. Now you like *him?*

I rolled my eyes at my inner voice.

I don't exactly make it a habit of letting people I dislike fuck me. Repeatedly.

The voice huffed, then went into the corner to pout.

Ha.

What I'd won, I wasn't certain. Because this argument could go on forever. We had a love/hate relationship. Sometimes he had good advice. Other times, he drove me nuts.

"You look very pensive." Malik pointed to my hot dog. "Regretting the relish and mustard?"

I shook my head. "Two of my favorite garnishes."

He wrinkled his nose. "Yeah, I'm ketchup all the way."

"Bland." I smiled, then bit into my hot dog.

"Each to their own." He bit into his.

We consumed them in silence, standing near a tree. A cool breeze came off the water, but nothing uncomfortable. *I think November is a crazy time to do this. What with the weather being so unpredictable. Still, this is an amazing turnout.*

Families as far as I could see. And lots of bikers in leather. I swallowed the last of my dog, scrunched up the paper wrapper, and tossed it into a recycling bin. "Do you come every year?"

Malik shook his head. "First time."

I eyed him. "So you had no idea how this would turn out."

"What's not to love? Junk food, rock band, and raising money. This is how to make a difference."

He wasn't wrong. A percentage of everything we bought would go to the charity, and I also planned to make a decent-sized donation tonight when I was on my computer. "That's a fair assessment." I sipped my cola. "But I'd say Razor Made—" I glanced around to ensure we were alone.

Relatively, we were. No one within hearing range.

"—are better than these guys." I pointed to the four men on the makeshift stage.

Malik grinned. "Ah, so you've listened to my music."

I rolled my eyes. "You think I wasn't going to investigate the troublemaker?"

He did a casual shrug. "Some people would've just told me to fuck off."

"Tempting."

His eyes widened.

I nudge his biceps with mine. "I'm here, aren't I? You slept in my bed."

"First guy to do that in your place, right?" He had a little self-satisfied, smug grin on his face.

Lying felt wrong. "You know you were. And definitely the first to hunker down with both Moses and me." Because I'd rescued the cat *after* the falling-out with Paul. Well, getting dumped.

"A threesome I will never forget." He grabbed my now-empty cola can and dropped it, along with his, into the appropriate recycling bin. Then he linked arms with me. "I want to try to win a stuffed animal for you."

"That's not really—"

"I'm certain Moses would love a furry friend. Shall I try for a squirrel?"

I laughed. I'd told him about Moses's penchant for sitting at the sliding glass door and chirping at any and all birds and squirrels who appeared either on the balcony or on the trees just behind the condo. "Yes, he'd love a furry friend." I couldn't be certain. What I knew about Moses was his love of feather dusters and laser pointers. Everything else was a crapshoot. Oh, and catnip. He adored catnip.

"Great." Malik led me over to a ring toss.

Eight minutes later, I carried a giant stuffed squirrel over to the cotton-candy stand. He bought us a swirl of blue-and-pink sugary goodness along with two bottles of water. We wandered close to the bandstand and listened as the group played another song which, although good, wasn't great. Half the time, I didn't understand the lyrics.

Malik whispered in my ear. "I have a song for you."

My stomach did a little flip-flop.

"Well, for TLIO."

I tamped down the disappointment. *Of course he didn't write a song for you. You're just one in a long line of people he's taken to his bed.* Damn, my inner voice was probably right. Although I'd shared my dearth of partners with him, he'd never reciprocated. I decided I probably didn't want to know. "Really? I can't wait to hear it."

"Conveniently, I have my acoustic guitar in my trunk. I'm happy to give you a private show. Your house or mine?"

I blinked as he met my gaze. The one thing he'd made clear was he never brought his hookups back to his place. He didn't want them getting ideas about his wealth. From what he'd said, much of it was tied in the real estate. He worked part-time to cover many of his expenses. I hadn't asked if record sales were great because, truly, none of my business.

"Moses will be upset. He'll be expecting dinner."

"We could feed him and then head to my place. He'd be okay for a few hours, right?" His eyes darkened. "Or a night?" Apparently with desire.

This is a big step. It's one thing to listen to his song. It's another entirely to go to his house.

I shoved my doubts aside. "Sure, we can do that. I'll need to be home early in the morning, though."

"No worries." He pecked my lips.

I tasted the gritty sugar. I also loved that we could do this in public. Vancouver was an accepting city—for the most part. I'd certainly never experienced overt bigotry. That said, I didn't tend to do PDA. For Malik, I'd make an exception. "Shall we head out?"

He grinned. "Yeah. Let's."

So we did.

Chapter Eighteen

Malik

I worried about inviting Spencer into my house.

He barely batted an eyelash. Whether I'd adequately prepared him, whether he'd researched my family, or whether he simply assumed all rock stars lived lavish lifestyles, I couldn't be certain.

We stopped to feed Moses—who dove into his food and paid us no mind—then headed to my place. On the way, though, nerves got the best of me. "See...this is what we should be doing—noise and chaos and fun. Like this afternoon."

He covered his laugh with a clearing of his throat. He obviously thought he could fool me.

Not possible.

I was getting to know him. His quirks, his tells, and his emotions. Far more than I ever would've thought possible.

At a red light, I gazed over at him.

He smiled. "I half expected you to pick up a guitar and start jamming with them."

"Ah, you know me well." The light turned green. I checked both ways before advancing into the intersection. "I didn't know those folks, and it would've been incredibly presumptuous of me to just hop on stage."

"You do sort of have more talent than them.

I grinned. "Is that a compliment?"

He cleared his throat again—almost like telling the truth was painful. "Yeah, I guess it is."

"And you'll let me play the song for you?"

"Sure. I guess so. Although I think Bonnie and Blossom should hear it as well."

"You don't trust your judgement?"

"I'm not necessarily your target audience."

I turned right on West 16th Avenue. Soon, I hung a left on Yew Street. Headed south, I tried not to pay attention to how many of the houses were so much bigger than most in Spencer's neighborhood.

After heading down West 22nd Ave, I cut down Valley Drive for a block and then headed into the back alley leading to my house.

Spencer's silence unnerved me. *Was I supposed to react to his target audience comment? Was he implying he was too old? I was too young? Maybe too immature? And, most importantly, what's he going to think of the house?* I pressed the remote, and my garage door slid open. Once my SUV was safely inside, I cut the engine and pressed the remote. As always, I watched carefully until the door was down.

"Are you okay?"

Spencer's words startled me, and I gazed over at him. "What do you mean?"

"I've sat here for the last couple of miles, watching you grip the steering wheel tighter and tighter. One would think you weren't happy bringing me here. I can hop a bus home and—"

"No." I nearly shouted the word, and it reverberated in the confined space of my vehicle. "Let me plug in the charger, and then we can head inside."

He telegraphed his movement as he reached his left hand out to place on my right—still gripping the steering wheel.

Slowly I released my grip, then laced my fingers with his. *He can feel my sweaty palms.* "I come across as a guy who's got his shit together. That's...not always the case."

"You don't bring people here."

I shook my head. "I don't want them to get the wrong impression."

"Well, let's lay our cards on the table—what impression are you wanting to give me?"

His words caught me off guard. What was my purpose for bringing him here? I wasn't certain. Still, I owed him some kind of an explanation. "Maybe I want to sing you the song in the recording studio?"

"Okay."

"Maybe I want to show off my house?"

"Sure." He didn't sound convinced with that word.

"Perhaps I want to share a king-sized bed with just you? No cat?"

He grinned. "On Moses's behalf, I should be offended. Alas, I'm not. Even right now, he's spread across my bed like a king on a large divan. We all know who really runs my house."

"Your tiny cat?"

"Yep. As many pet owners discover—our companions often rule the roost."

"Well, that's good to know. I've never had a pet, as I told you."

"Have you considered getting one?"

"I'm often out of the house for long days. We've done a couple of small tours. It's not like I can take a dog or cat with me."

He appeared to consider. "That's probably true. Although if musicians can take their children with them on the road, I don't see why they couldn't take their pets." He squeezed my hand. "Now, are you showing me your house, or am I grabbing a bus back to Moses?"

I grinned. "Okay, come on in." I released his hand and hopped out of the vehicle. While I plugged in the charger, he retrieved my guitar from the back seat.

Without being asked.

His quiet consideration often got to me. He put others before himself for much of the time. Without expectations of reciprocity. In fact, he was uncomfortable when people offered to take care of him. *I want to change that.*

Once the charger was set, I beckoned him toward the door. "The garage faces the alley, and it's bordered by a high fence—so people can't sneak in the back way." We stepped into the backyard and I set the alarm before I closed the door, ensuring the thing was locked. "The paranoia was mostly my father's, but it stuck with me. Everything is alarmed." Even as I said the words, the back floodlights turned on.

Spencer shielded his eyes. "Christ, that's bright."

I panicked with my heart rate galloping. "I'm so sorry—I didn't think. I can't turn them off." I groped for his hand. "Follow me into the house." I yanked.

"I'm all right, Malik. Just...unexpected." Still, he didn't lower his hand and instead allowed me to guide him. Once we were at the back door, and out of the bright lights, he dropped my hand.

I fumbled with my keys, but managed to get the door unlocked. I stepped inside and killed the alarm. "So sorry."

The light in the back hallway wasn't as bright, thank God.

I took my guitar from him.

"You don't have to apologize. Bright lights don't always trigger a headache."

I eyed him. "Did it this time?"

He shook his head.

Inwardly, I breathed a sigh of relief. "Can I get you something to drink? To eat? Lunch was a while ago." After we'd finished our hot dogs, we'd wandered through the park, taking in all the sights. We'd even wandered over to the motorcycles. I knew more about bikes, and would've stayed longer, but clearly Spencer hadn't been interested. Oh, he'd feigned interest—but I knew him better. In the end, as dusk had set in, we'd made our way to his place.

Moses had a huge stuffed squirrel to play with and a full belly.

I had Spencer.

Somehow, I got the better end of that deal. "Do you want to take your coat off? I don't keep the place too warm, unless it's freezing out, but—"

He shrugged out of his coat and hung it in the coat closet.

I put the guitar case down on the hardwood floor and did the same thing. Then I straightened. "So. Uh...food? Tour? Music?" *Why do I feel so nervous? Oh, right. Because I never bring anyone here. Certainly no one I care about.* That thought brought me up short. It shouldn't have—but it did. I cared about Spencer. No two ways about it. He'd become important to me. His opinion mattered. I still thought he was a bit of a stuffed shirt...but he was growing on me. As time marched on, I saw less of my father and his disapproval. Spencer...he wanted to make me a better person. My father had simply wanted to browbeat me into submission.

Spencer placed a hand on my arm. "I'm not really hungry yet—hot dog, cotton candy, and popcorn was a lot."

"Yeah. Amazing we didn't get tummy aches."

He grinned. "Yes, a throwback to childhood. Why don't you give me a tour that culminates in the recording studio? Then, if we're hungry, we can eat something light."

"Uh..." I squinted. "Just about everything's frozen. If you want to eat it, we might consider unfreezing it or putting it on to cook now."

"Oh." He pursed his lips. "What were you planning for dinner?"

You.

Somehow, though, I was pretty sure that wasn't what he meant. "I don't have plans."

"So we could do a salad?" He grinned. "You should see your face."

"Hey, I eat salad."

He arched an eyebrow.

I pursed my lips. "Okay, not recently. I mean, I ate healthy from the café."

"That was days ago." He linked his arm in mine. "Let's check out what you've got in the kitchen."

Deciding we could circle back for the guitar, I guided him into the massive kitchen. The family room was part of the colossal space. I pointed. "Dining room is in there. Very formal. I never use it." Well, almost never. I pointed toward another archway. "Living room. Very formal. I never use it."

He grinned. "So you like it here? It's..." He spun around.

"Not cozy?"

"Well, I wasn't going to say that. I think you could fit my entire condo in this space."

The kitchen and living room combo ran the length of the back of the house. "You're probably not off with that estimation. The primary suite is directly above here and the same size."

He gaped.

"Well, just about. That includes two walk-in closets that are each bigger than your sleeping area, a five-piece bathroom, and a lounging room."

"You have an entire room for lounging?"

"Northeast corner. You can see some wicked sunrises."

He pointed to the back of the house. "North facing?"

I nodded. "Still gets plenty of light. The front foyer is two stories with massive glass windows. We look out over Trafalgar Park. My parents bought this house for the prestige—but didn't factor in the noise of the park. We rarely opened windows on the south side of the house."

"Sheesh. I love the noise kids…" He trailed off. "I wouldn't keep the windows closed. Especially if there's a nice breeze. Nothing like airing the house out."

I paused, my hand on the handle of the freezer. "Does it feel stale?"

He shook his head. "Far from it. Just…I love fresh air. Admittedly, city air isn't the cleanest, but when the wind blows in off the Georgia Strait and brings the tang of water? There's just something to that."

Something I'd never considered. "Yeah." I opened the freezer. "Oh, how about some flatbread? There's a vegetarian option." I wrinkled my nose before I realized how that might look. Then I tried to school my expression.

He rolled his eyes, then grabbed the package. "We just have to preheat the over and cook for twelve minutes. That won't take much time. So tour, music, then yeah, we can come back here and this looks just perfect for dinner—not too heavy." He winked. "And vegetarian."

Something inside me warmed a bit. "Tour?"

He nodded.

Then reached for my hand.

I guided him through the formal dining room and then across to the equally formal living room. I stood at the entryway for my father's study as he poked his head in. Next, I took him up the stairs. First to the bedroom my mother had converted to her office.

Again, I stood in the entryway.

Then came the three spare bedrooms and three lavish bathrooms.

He gaped. "Seriously?"

I grinned. "Wait until you see mine." I led him that way and flipped on the light as he entered.

"I'm impressed."

"Why? The size?"

"No." He turned to face me. "I expected..."

"Dirty?"

"Well, no. More...chaotic."

"Everything has a place and all that." I leaned against the door frame as he examined my bookcase. "I still expect my mother to perform an inspection. And since she always reported her findings to my father, my rebellious phase lasted about—" I scratched my chin. "Twenty minutes...?"

He snickered. Then sobered. "This must be hard."

Clearly, he didn't mean keeping a clean room. "I have someone who comes once a week to clean, do laundry, and make a few meals. I don't want to burden her, so I do my best."

"Have you ever done your own laundry?"

"Um... Is there a right way to answer that?"

"What if you spill sauce on your favorite shirt and you want to wear it again before laundry day?"

I grinned and pointed to the walk-in closet.

He walked in and guffawed. He poked his head back out. "Seriously?"

"If I see something I like, I buy a few of them. That way I never have to worry. It also means I'm less likely to wear things out."

"Those jeans..." He pointed to my legs.

"Well, jeans are an exception. If I find a pair I like, I'll wear them until they disintegrate."

"That's...a choice." He grinned. Then pointed to the bathroom while arching an eyebrow.

"Go ahead."

He walked inside and this time whistled. "Seriously?" He shook his head again. "How much space does one person need?"

"Is there a right answer to that?" This time I was a little less flippant. A little more soulful.

"It must get lonely."

I shrugged. "I was lonely when they were alive. It's why I had friends over as often as I could get away with."

"But not now?"

"It's not that simple. When I joined the orchestra, my high school friends sort of slipped away. University, dating...all that stuff. I had my music to focus on and, frankly, the friends I made there weren't the type to come over and hang around. From there..." Another shrug. "Until I met Creed, I was lost. He comes over plenty. Along with Reese and Freddie. I've even had Mama Murthi over for dinner. Catered, I promise. No way was I going to risk burning something to feed her."

"Would she have really minded?"

His question caught me off guard. "I guess... No, probably not. We also ate at the dining table, and I had the impression none of the grandeur impressed her. She wanted to see the spaces where I hung out."

"Same here." He stepped toward me. "So show me."

I grinned. "Yeah, okay." I grasped his hand and headed toward the stairs. Just before I led him down, though, I stopped. I pointed to a closed door. "That's their room. Was their room," I corrected.

"Ah."

"I haven't—" I swallowed.

"It's okay." He pressed a hand over my heart.

"I should probably... I mean... I'm the head of the house now, right? So I should, you know—" I swallowed again.

"Who says?" He met my gaze, his eyes dark green in the low light. "There's no hard-and-fast rule. Given the size of your bedroom—and your bed—I'd say you're just fine in there."

"Yeah." I wanted to make some glib joke about my bed, but this moment felt too tenuous. Too precious. Too perilous. "The lady who cleans the house goes in there every month. Or so I think. It should be clean—" I'd never checked. I probably should have...but I hadn't.

"Do you want me to check?"

His offer touched me. And alleviated a knot in my chest. "Would you? I don't know what I'll do if you say there's a layer of dust—" I bit my lip.

"How about I check, and we cross that bridge when we come to it?"

I nodded. Sound reasoning. Very logical. Just one of the many things I liked about him.

He released me. Then, slowly, he turned the knob. With one final glance in my direction, he headed into their room.

The urge to look seized me, then, just as quickly, passed. I moved to the top of the stairs and dropped. The grand staircase was before me. Halfway down, it cleaved in half and curved downward in two pieces. The foyer was two stories of windows. On sunny days, this space was drenched in sunlight. Almost overwhelmingly so. We rarely used the front door, so if that doorbell rang, the visitor was likely a stranger.

A door shut and Spencer plopped next to me.

I linked my arm through his and leaned against him.

"Not a speck of dust. All the clothes hanging in the closet are in dry cleaner bags. I didn't open the drawers, but I suspect as much care was taken with them. The bathroom's spotless. Whoever does your cleaning is doing a good job."

I blinked. "Thank you for that."

He shrugged. "Not much to do. That space is...massive. I can see why it might feel like a waste to leave so much of the house unused."

I waited, but nothing more was forthcoming. "Do you think I should move in there?"

A long time passed before he drew in a long breath and let it out slowly. "Only you can answer that question. I don't have a lot of experience with grief—certainly nothing as profound as losing a parent. Let alone two. I think—" He cleared his throat. "I know a charity that accepts donations of professional clothes. They give them to people trying to enter the workforce who've faced barriers—poverty, incarceration, addiction—things that make getting a job much harder. At least they can go into interviews with nice clothes." He rested his ear against the top of my head that was resting on his shoulder. "Just something to consider. I can't see you wearing their clothes."

I laughed. Lightheartedly. "No. Definitely not. Both were much shorter than me. And I'd never feel right. But giving their clothes away? That feels...macabre."

"Then don't. It's just a suggestion. You might also find a consignment store. Then you could make some money."

I shivered. "That would be a hundred times worse. I don't need the money." I let the first suggestion settle over me. People who might benefit from my parents' things. Their very expensive and well-maintained clothes. That held some appeal. "Can you get me the number of those people? The ones who help people get back on their feet?"

"Sure. There's no rush. Some of those clothes are classic—they're not going to go out of fashion."

"That's true. I have my mother's jewelry. My father's cufflinks...." I swallowed again.

"Sentimental things you could easily pass along to your children."

"My—" I nearly swallowed my tongue. I pulled my head away from him and met his startled gaze—all wide eyes and confusion. "You think I'm going to have kids?"

He cocked his head. "You're young, Malik. I mean, you might know you're not going to have kids, which is fine. Or you might change your mind later. But..." He broke my gaze.

Gently, I pressed my fingers to his jaw and urged him to turn toward me.

To meet my gaze.

His eyes shone.

"Oh, sweetheart."

He sniffed. "It's stupid. Some people just aren't meant to be parents."

"But you wanted to be."

He swallowed. "Yeah, I did. I thought that Paul would come around to the idea..." He snickered. "More fool me."

"Jackass."

"Yeah, pretty much."

"You're only forty—that's not too late."

"With a job that barely keeps a roof over my head? With a five-hundred-square-foot condo?"

I nodded. "We make choices. This Land is Ours is your penance. I get it. But if you really want kids, you either need to marry someone rich or find a way to make more money. Or move to the middle of nowhere—but then you'd have employment problems." I winked. "Or marry a guy with a massive house and a decent inheritance."

He stilled.

I stilled. "I was just..."

"Yeah. I know." He blinked. "Music? Then we can eat. I'm getting hungry. Then—" He gestured to my bedroom with his chin.

I grinned. "Yeah. That."

With the moment of solemnity passed, we headed downstairs.

Chapter Nineteen

Spencer

I plopped onto the center of a massive black leather u-shaped couch.

Malik sat on a chair facing me and strummed out the song on his acoustic guitar. He didn't need sheet music or even a piece of paper with lyrics. He knew everything by heart.

Speaking of hearts...mine stuttered. His words were sung softly but with surety. His voice was both strong and gentle at the same time. The song built in intensity until it hit a crescendo...and then backed down to quiet again.

I blinked repeatedly. *Pike...you would've loved this. This would've been your anthem. This song would've inspired you.*

Malik finished singing, and the last chord faded. He tapped the body of the guitar and, finally, glanced up.

Our gazes held.

"Shit." He winced. "I didn't think it was that bad."

I cocked my head even as I blinked.

"You're crying."

At first, I didn't understand. *Is he really that uncertain of himself? Of his talent? Where's the arrogant asshole who knows everything?* "That was..." I leaned forward. "Your talent truly is remarkable. You captured what we're trying to do in a five-minute song."

"Well, three-and-a-half. It felt that long?"

"In a good way. I didn't want the song to end. I wanted to know what came next. What a brilliant idea you had."

"Group effort."

Again, I cocked my head.

He did some weird thing with his head that I couldn't quite interpret—not a shake, nor a nod. "Okay...mostly me. Reese did some of the melody, and she's got some ideas of what we can do if we go full orchestration."

"Or you can just have a solo voice and a lone guitar." I was curious what the song would sound like with Razor Made performing it—but I had also been completely captivated by just Malk's raw voice and the solo acoustic guitar. "Wow."

His gaze held mine. "Yeah?"

"I'm no expert...what did Reese, Creed, and Freddie think?"

"They loved it. Creed insisted I play it for Mama Murthi, and she said the song was one of my best compositions. I think she's a little biased."

"Is that Creed's mother?"

He nodded.

"Wouldn't she be more biased if Creed had written the song?"

He scrunched his nose—which he did when he was deep in thought. "I guess..."

I pushed up off the couch and made my way over to him. Gently, I removed the guitar from his hands and put it on the stand. Then I eased myself onto his lap—much as I had nearly a week ago. A moment of intimacy forever seared in my mind. I liked being in his lap—far more than I was willing to either admit or examine.

His stomach rumbled.

I pressed my forehead against his neck. "Dinner?"

"Yeah." He banded his arms around me. "In a minute or two."

How long we stayed that way, I couldn't have said.

A moment suspended in time.

We baked flatbread and ate watching the news.

We cuddled in his bed and made love for hours.

After breakfast, we went back to my place.

He played guitar while I sucked up to my severely annoyed cat.

I prepared my presentation while he dozed.

Just a lazy Sunday afternoon.

Dinner was at a Thai place down the street that served the most amazing vegan Thai red curry with tofu.

Our eyes watered.

We brushed our teeth before falling into bed and making love repeatedly.

Every time we came together, I swore it was better than the last. He was learning my body and what made me feel good. I figured out what made him tick and what got his engine revving.

Monday morning came too early—in the guise of a cat sitting on my face.

"Is that comfortable?" Malik's voice carried quite a bit of humor.

"It's his way of telling me he's hungry." Gently, I moved Moses off my face.

"Well, it got you to stop snoring."

I shot Malik a murderous glance.

He grinned, kissed my nose, and got out of bed. He headed to the bathroom—offering me the most glorious view of his very fine ass. He jiggled it just before he disappeared.

I groaned. "Do that and I'll never make my meeting."

A chuckle came just before he closed the bathroom door.

I glared at Moses. "I might've gotten lucky."

He blinked—clearly indicating he didn't give a shit and could I please hurry up and feed him?

Slowly, I rolled out of bed. My ass was just the right kind of sore as we'd...fucked...a whole pile of times. He never seemed to run out of stamina. My cock was always willing to rouse. I couldn't remember ever being this horny. Given I'd been sleeping with guys for a long time, that lack of memory niggled. *You're not remembering because you have sex brain. Best ever means no one else counts. Certainly not Paul Fuck Face.*

Malik's new nickname for my ex.

Moses twined himself between my legs as I emptied a perfect portion of wet food for him. He purred loudly and dug in as I moved to my laptop.

"You're working?"

Hand pressed to my heart—I spun to find a very naked Malik at the other end of my galley kitchen. "You scared me.

"I came to invite you to have a shower with me." He offered the lascivious grin I'd come to love. He crooked a finger.

Of course I followed him.

Ten minutes later, sated between the mutual hand jobs, we lathered up. "So, Saturday was your day, right?"

He eyed me as he wet his hair. He'd brought something to put in it later, he'd explained. "Sure."

"Well, why don't you come with me today? See my point of view?"

An eyebrow arched as he shampooed his hair.

I rotated us so the spray ran down my back. I shimmied a bit to try to get the soap out of my nooks and crevices.

"You said you're meeting with a member of Parliament."

"I am." I wet my hair—which admittedly took way less time.

"Sounds boring."

I dumped a dollop of shampoo into my hand, then lathered up my hair. "You say that, but I'm also visiting North Vancouver and the First Nation over there."

His eyes widened in interest. "Yeah, okay."

"You have to promise to behave."

Those eyes narrowed. "When am I not behaved?"

For my part, I rolled my eyes.

Eventually we dried, styled our hair, ate breakfast, and headed out the door.

Malik worried because he wore jeans, a nice shirt, and a leather jacket.

I assured him he'd be fine.

He was.

During my meeting with my MP, he hung out in the reception area and entertained her staff.

I rolled my eyes yet again, but was pleased when she asked him for an autograph—for her grandchildren.

He was thrilled to do that...and grabbed a CD, signing that as well.

While I met with indigenous band members in North Vancouver, about what TLIO could do to coordinate with them on several pressing issues, Malik joined a guided hike around the area. He should've worn more appropriate footwear, but I hadn't been certain how the day would progress. With the brilliant sunshine and mild temperatures, pretty much everyone who wasn't in our meeting wanted to be outside.

On our ride back across the Lion's Gate Bridge, he continued enthusing.

I sat back and let his words wash over me. I tried not to think about how much work I'd created for myself during my two meetings today.

"...so cool." He sighed. "Counterflow."

I laughed. "We're heading *into* Downtown Vancouver while the bulk of the commuters are headed home to North and West Vancouver. We'll survive."

"At least my vehicle is electric."

I patted his knee. "You've done all right."

"Today was enlightening. I didn't know the band's history before. I was...humbled."

"That happens. One of my distant, distant, distant relations wrote a guidebook to fells in the Lake District in England. My family came to Canada over a hundred years ago, but I'm well aware we're newcomers."

"Like, I'd never heard of Triquet Island." He tapped his hand on the steering wheel. "The settlement they found? Fourteen-thousand years old. That's three times older than the pyramids."

"That is cool." I clutched my messenger bag as a huge SUV in the counterflow lane came awfully close to us. "So you heard about the six-thousand-year-old arrowhead they found up near Williams Lake?"

"Right. Closer, though, is the Matsqui First Nation. Out near Mission City? Nine thousand years." He nodded. "And Tsleil-Waututh, Squamish, and Musqueam first nations? Around this area...?" His hand swung from the windshield where Stanley Park approached back to North Van where we'd just come from. "I learned about this stuff in school, but..." He tapped the steering wheel. "I almost feel like it's not my story to tell. Not my song to sing."

I wasn't certain how to answer that. "You're not trying to take someone's identity. To tell the story as if it's your own." I tried to let that sit.

"But my perspective might be different because of my cultural heritage?" He eyed the GPS. "Every route between here and your place is red."

"We could stop and eat at White Spot for dinner. Wait until traffic thins before we head home."

"Moses?" He glanced at the GPS again as we inched through the magnificent Stanely Park.

"Will not starve. Plenty of nights I've worked late, and he hasn't expired. He's got kibble. He knows how to eat it—he just chooses not to."

"Would you if you had the choice?"

As we came around the causeway bend that turned into West Georgia Street, we picked up a bit of speed.

"I eat plenty of things I'd rather not."

"Ha." He signaled to pull into the restaurant parking lot. He selected a spot, parked, killed the engine, but didn't get out.

I held myself still.

"I've faced discrimination."

"Yep."

"My family came north on the underground railroad. From Georgia."

I waited. I hadn't asked and maybe that had been a mistake. I just figured he'd tell me when he was ready. Apparently he was ready.

"Canada offered the opportunity to be free, but true equality...?" He cleared his throat. "We've had a bunch of Black folks doing firsts.

One day I'd like that to end. I would hope that my people would have done everything that everyone else has done. You know what I mean?"

"I think you mean that you'd rather someone be known for their accomplishment and not the color of their skin or their heritage." *Sheesh, am I saying the right thing?* "Not color blind. Just that..."

"Yeah. That. I'll always be Black. If I have kids who are like me, they'll be Black. I just don't want them to go through what I went through. If I live where I live and they go to the same school..." He scratched his jaw. "But does it really matter?"

"You're asking if a more ethnically diverse neighborhood might lead to less bullying? I don't know." I wracked my brain for the right words. "I think kids will always bully other kids. If not for the color of their skin, then the clothes they wear, the accent they have, or something none of us can predict. You teach your kids—" My voice caught. "You give them all the tools in the world to be brave and strong. To be resistant to the insults while, simultaneously, ensuring they don't bully other kids. Either accidentally or intentionally. Childhood sucks, Malik. You can do everything right and your child still gets hurt. Resiliency means being able to get back up after being knocked down.

"You're resilient. You're one of the most resilient people I know." I rested my hand on his thigh. "You survived childhood and then the loss of your parents. You left security and forged the path you wanted to. That's important. And, I mean, you've got goals and shit—"

"Rocktoberfest."

"—yeah, that. So keep looking forward."

He met my gaze. Night had fallen and only a lamp in the parking lot illuminated us—with a weird pink glow.

"Today really opened my eyes."

I had no doubt. I remembered my first visit to the First Nation. Talk about a resilient people. "Well, see? We don't need two-hundred bikers and a thousand-person picnic everywhere. Sometimes we let nature—and the people we're trying to help—guide us. I would never presume to speak on behalf of someone—be they Indigenous, Black, Asian, or anyone else. Acknowledging the wrong is part of the solution, I know. So I do the land acknowledgements. I welcome diverse opinions. I'm on a journey."

"It's not easy." He placed his hand on mine. "I have moments..."

I held my breath.

"I'm hungry. I want a steak or ribs or something."

A snicker escaped my lips.

He leaned over and kissed me. When he pulled back, I caught a gleam in his dark-brown eyes. "What are you having?"

"Either the Avocado Impossible Burger or the Brie and Mushroom veggie burger." I grinned. "You know, they're both amazing."

He arched an eyebrow. "Fungi?"

"Yum."

"I'll try the avocado burger thingy." He sighed dramatically.

I kissed his cheek.

Hours later, as we lay in my bed, Moses tried to play with a sleeping Malik's hair.

Knowing distraction worked, I hauled my cat over to my side of the bed and encouraged him to sleep on my pillow. Then I pulled Malik into my arms and hoped fervently all his dreams would come true.

Chapter Twenty

Malik

November was a blur of working at the studio, rehearsing with the band, and being with Spencer every possible moment in between.

December was more chaos as the deadline for our Rocktoberfest application was nearing. The studio's calendar was full, and I was getting plenty of work. Cramming in more rehearsals was a challenge.

Reese worked retail—so this was her busiest time of year.

Freddie worked for a delivery service and was up to his eyeballs whenever he signed on for a shift. He made a ton of money in tips, but the work was grueling, and his stress was high as he had tight deadlines.

Mama Murthi was especially busy this year—her legal-aid docket completely jam-packed. She recruited Creed to do administrative work for her. Which freed up her time to visit with clients while having the side benefit of keeping her *trouble child* out of mischief.

Well, that was the intention.

It mostly worked.

Still, Creed was spending an inordinate amount of time in my basement studio. Ostensibly working on new music. In reality, he was hiding out from his mother.

I was supportive. To a point.

On the evening of the twenty-first, he and I jammed while Spencer sat on the sectional black leather sofa with his laptop. His brow was furrowed in concentration. He also wore his reading glasses—newly prescribed by the optometrist I'd insisted he see. The glasses hadn't helped with the migraines—which were still too frequent, as far as I was concerned—but he had fewer tension headaches. Likely from less squinting.

Score one for me.

He rode me hard about getting my shit together music-wise and to stop focusing on social media. I'd written three more songs.

Score one for Spencer.

Creed stopped drumming.

I stopped strumming.

Spencer gazed up. He met my eyes, nodded as if realizing everything was okay, then went back to his laptop. He'd tried to explain it to me—some new legislation. He was tearing it apart and sending copious emails to his Member of Parliament. As if she, one of three-hundred-and-forty-three, could somehow impact the legislation. He was prepared to email all of them if it meant he got his way.

I both admired him and was terrified of him. I had a business lawyer who had never steered me wrong. I had an estate attorney who worked her ass off to keep everything running smoothly.

Still, I trusted Spencer more than both of them combined—even though contract and real estate law weren't his specialty.

He also loved hot chocolate, so I made that for him frequently.

I sipped my water as my phone buzzed with an incoming call. I glanced at the screen and nearly dropped the phone.

Pauletta Magnum.

"Holy shit."

The panic in my voice must've reached my companions.

Creed was up from his drums and at my side in the space of a ring.

Two more and Spencer was on my other side.

"Dude, you've got to answer that." Creed pointed to my phone. "It's Pauletta Fucking Magnum. You do not want this call to go to voicemail."

I met Spencer's gaze. While his eyes were wide with confusion, he pressed himself against me—offering unspoken support.

I pressed to accept the call, then put it on speakerphone. "Hello?" My voice cracked. Because of course it did. I cleared my throat. "This is Malik Forestal."

"Oh, good." A strong voice carried through the line. "I never know when I track down a phone number if it's the right one. You're not an easy man to find, Mr. Forestal."

If I'd known you were looking for me, I wouldn't have hidden myself so well.

"Apologies."

"No worries. When you're famous, you'll be glad you're tough to reach."

"Famous?" My voice came out as a croak.

"Well, bigger than you are now. I have plans for you. First, though, I should introduce myself. My name is Pauletta Magnum. You might know that I rep Grindstone."

"Yes ma'am. I'm aware." She'd helped them land a huge contract with Grand Central Records. Well, their talent caught the recording label's notice. But she'd negotiated the contract. At least that was my memory of what I'd heard through the grapevine. "May I ask why you're calling me?"

Creed rolled his eyes.

Spencer gripped my arm. Thankfully the one *not* holding the phone.

"I saw your concert last month."

I wracked my mind. We'd done two. One at a dive bar just off Commercial Drive and one at The Pearl. "Oh?"

"You were the opening act. Way better than the headlining band."

I'd thought the same thing, but never would've said it. I had just been grateful for the opportunity to play at a real venue.

Mama Murthi and Spencer had worked our merch table, and we'd sold out of CDs and most of our T-shirts. Not bad for being the opening act.

I cleared my throat. "Well, at least you saw one of our better performances."

Creed groaned.

I shot him a look.

Spencer tightened his grip on my arm.

"Yes, well." A moment passed. "I've heard you're hit and miss. More hits than misses, but you need work. Refinement. Control."

She wasn't saying anything I didn't already know. We were good. We could be better. We needed to be at the top of our game to get to Rocktoberfest.

"I want to rep you."

Creed pumped his fist in the air.

"What's the catch?" Because there was always a catch. Top-notch agents didn't just call out of the blue and offer to rep. *At least she's heard you play.*

"You know I plucked Grindstone out of obscurity and made them stars."

"Sure." *Where is she going with this?*

"That took years. Raw talent but no discipline. Axel and Ed also needed to find the right keyboardist, drummer, and bassist."

"My band is my family. I'm not doing any of this without—"

"Relax." She chuckled. "You've got a good band together already. But you need...more."

"So you said. What do you suggest?"

"I'd like to meet with you in person before giving you the pitch."

That sounds ominous. "Look, Ms. Magnum. You're busy. We're busy. Why don't you say what you have to say, and then we can decide whether or not to meet."

Again, she chuckled. "Persistent. I like that. I have someone willing to work with you. An award-winning producer. But...it's complicated."

Creed and I exchanged glances.

I checked the time on my phone. "Creed's already here. Reese and Freddie are due in an hour. Our lawyer's here as well."

Spencer coughed.

"That's an interesting turn." Pauletta's voice came across as amused.

Creed rolled his eyes.

"Well, he's not my entertainment lawyer."

"Just your boyfriend?"

I nearly dropped the phone.

Pauletta chuckled for the third time. "I caught sight of you and Spencer Wainright getting...close. I do my research, Malik. I want to know who I'm offering to rep. If any of you have skeletons in the closet, you're better off telling me now."

The documentary about Grindstone flashed in my mind. How ten years ago, Axel's girlfriend had overdosed when he'd been in rehab. How they'd kept the secret to themselves until a documentary film-maker—the woman's brother—had forced the truth to surface. How Ed and Axel had lived clean lives and stayed away from drugs and booze. How they encouraged their fans to do the same thing.

"I don't have any, Pauletta." I held Creed's gaze.

He shook his head.

"I don't have any reason to believe any of my bandmates do either."

"Great. I can be there in an hour. I have contracts which, of course, you'll want your lawyer to read."

Spencer could look them over tonight, and Gemma could tear them apart tomorrow before we signed. *Better call her and give her the heads-up.* I rattled off my address.

"Nice neighborhood. I don't live too far away."

"It's a long story."

"No doubt." She paused. "May I bring Mickey? They're my partner. And a documentary film producer. I don't have any plans to film you, but they've always got a good sense for people and often bring great ideas to the table."

A nonbinary partner? Interesting. "Of course they're welcome here. See you in an hour. You can park on the street and ring the bell."

"See you then." She cut the connection.

I stared at Creed. "Uh...did you understand that?"

"Nope." He puffed out his chest. "*The* Pauletta Magnum, manager of the Grindstone, wants to rep us."

"Did you catch the bit about a producer?"

"An *award-winning* producer." Spencer finally released my hand and put his on his hips. "This sounds fishy."

Creed whacked him on the upper arm. Gently, but with meaning. "Let's hear what she has to say before we pass judgement. This might be a really good opportunity."

"Or she might demand you agree to work with this producer or she won't rep you." He scowled.

I held up my hand. "Let's not jump to any conclusions. Creed, you touch base with Freddie and make sure he's on the way. I'll do the same with Reese. I suggest we wait until they get here before we spring the Pauletta news on them."

"And Mickey." Spencer's brow creased. "That's not usual, is it? To bring a documentary producer to a contract meeting?"

"Are you staying?" I arched an eyebrow.

"Of course." Then he squinted. "If you want me to...?"

"Duh." Creed whacked him again. "You're a lawyer. She's bringing a contract."

"Yes, but as Malik pointed out, I'm neither a contract nor an entertainment lawyer. And he's also my boyfriend." He eyed me to be certain.

I nodded.

"So, conflicts of interest galore. I can sit in as his boyfriend, but I can't be his legal representation."

"Could you be mine?" Again, Creed puffed out his chest.

Spencer smiled and rolled his eyes. "Uh...no." He whacked Creed back on the biceps. "Good try, though."

I held up my phone.

Creed shrugged and sauntered off to the sound booth.

I texted Reese—her preferred method of communication.

A minute later, she gave me the thumbs up and a *ten mins out*.

"Hot chocolate." I snagged Spencer's hand and guided him upstairs.

"You're nervous." He followed me into the kitchen with a concerned expression—furrowed brow and all.

I snagged the jug of milk and a saucepan. "Reese will want one as well. Do you think I should make enough in case Mickey and/or Pauletta want some? I've got the coffee machine—"

He placed his hands over mine, gently guiding me to put the milk and saucepan on the counter. He took my hands and pulled me into his arms. "Whatever this is, it'll be over in a couple of hours. You're free to take your time making the decision. You're a band of four, so there'll be a discussion. I know this seems like a really big deal—"

"This is Pauletta Fucking Magnum. She made Grindstone."

"Yes. You showed me the documentary. Really impressive. But they were ten-years-in-the-making overnight successes."

"She's better at her job now. She's got connections. She can help us with our Rocktoberfest demo."

"That's all true. But you also have to stay true to who you are. And that means listening, taking it in, and deciding as a band. Don't rush to judgement. Don't jump headfirst without testing the depth of the water."

I chuckled. "Is that really a saying? Isn't it something about feet-first?"

"Well, if the water's shallow and you jump in headfirst, I'd say you're in big trouble."

I grasped his biceps. "Thank you."

"You're welcome." He kissed my lips. "Make extra hot chocolate. We can always have it for breakfast."

"Aren't we staying at your place tonight?"

He nodded. "Right. Moses."

I set about pouring the milk into the saucepan. "You know, we could set up a litter box for him here. For the nights you stay over.

Then he won't take his aggression out on that poor stuffed squirrel."
A squirrel we'd had to repair more than once.

"What do you mean?"

"We could make it even easier." I turned the burner on, then set the saucepan down.

He curled myself against me—taking me in his arms. "How?"

"Well, you could just, you know, be here. All the time." I held my breath.

He stilled.

For a very long time.

"Or not. It's a stupid suggestion. You'd be much farther away from work. And you've got your condo—"

"I'm allowed to rent it out." He pressed his nose against my ear. "Are you asking me to move in? It's only been two months."

I stirred the milk with the wooden spoon I'd grabbed. "Sure. Except either you're here or I'm there just about every night. I hate when we're apart. I don't like leaving the house empty, and Moses shouldn't be alone as often as he is." I took a deep breath. "Seems to me the solution is pretty simple."

"Dude." Creed sauntered into the kitchen. "Are you *finally* asking him to move in?"

I stopped my stirring and turned in Spencer's arms to face him. "Yeah. I am. The question is, will he accept my offer?"

Chapter Twenty-One

Spencer

I read the fear in his expression. He was worried I'd say *no*. That I'd reject him. At least here, I could reassure him. "Yes, I'll move in with you. We need to talk about Moses and all the precious things in this house—"

"He doesn't give a shit about any of that." Creed gestured to the stove with his chin. "Pay attention."

"Right. Shit." Malik resumed his stirring. "I should be jumping up and down for joy, right?"

"Did you think I'd say *no*?"

"I think you've got a good thing going. Ten-minute bike ride to the office—"

"And it's thirty-five minutes from here along the Seaside Bicycle Route." I shrugged. "Or it's forty-five minutes and two buses on transit."

"Or you could take your electric SUV. How long would the drive be?" He scrunched his nose. "I should know this."

"Peak rush hour? Forty-minutes."

"It might be quicker to bike." He continued to stir the hot chocolate.

Reluctantly, I let him go and made my way to the cupboard with the mugs. I gestured to Creed.

He grinned and nodded enthusiastically.

I pulled down seven. If anyone didn't want coffee, tea, or hot chocolate, we still had water, a few different kinds of soda, and milk.

We.

Funny how I felt so comfortable in this house. Yes, it was ten times larger than any place I'd ever lived in. Yes, it was formal and elegant and all these things I wasn't. Even my downtown condo, when I'd been working my corporate job, hadn't been anything like this mansion.

Yet, in this space with Malik, comfort enveloped me. Basically, we stuck to his bedroom, the kitchen and family room combination room, and the recording studio. Those were our happy places.

Move in? Is that wise?

I pursed my lips as I sorted out packets of tea we could offer.

Reese barreled into the room. "Oh my God, what's up? Freddie texted and said you were being all secretive. Oh, is that hot chocolate?"

Malik added more milk to the saucepan and continued stirring.

Creed slung his arm around Reese. "I might've made things sound more mysterious to get Freddie riled up and to light a fire under his ass."

Not a bad strategy. Freddie was, invariably, the last to arrive.

"I'm home." Freddie bellowed the words from the front door.

Everyone in the band had keys, and we turned the alarm off when we were expecting everyone. For all the fanciness of the house, there hadn't been any break-in attempts. Surely the multiple surveillance signs and the motion-activated lights would deter anyone. Someone brazen enough to try a daytime robbery was likely to be foiled as well.

Freddie strutted into the kitchen and dropped his knapsack on the floor.

I pointed. "Pick that up. We've got company coming." I turned to Malik. "Kitchen table or dining room, do you figure? Or something more comfortable?"

"You're thinking formal?" He cocked his head as he continued to stir the bubbling liquid.

"I think seven people can fit in the family room or the kitchen table. I think if you want a more of them versus us then the dining room makes more sense. Maybe you four on one side, Mickey and Pauletta on the other and maybe me at the head?"

"Switzerland?"

Freddie opened the fridge. "Who are Mickey and Pauletta..." He slammed the fridge door shut. "Pauletta? Like Pauletta Magnum?"

Malik grinned. "Yep."

Reese, who'd been dispensing the chocolate, paused. "Why is that name familiar?"

"Because she's Grindstone's manager?" Creed snatched the powdered chocolate before she dropped it.

"And she's coming here?" Reese might've squeaked that.

"Yep." I pointed to the coffee maker.

Everyone shook their heads.

Apparently I'd made hot chocolate converts of all of them.

Reese pressed a hand to her belly. "Why? What did she say?"

"She said she had something to present to us and she wanted to do it in person." Malik turned the burner off. "So that's five hot chocolates?"

Everyone else nodded.

Reese spooned chocolate powder into each mug and stood back as Malik poured milk into each. "There's enough for two more if that's what Pauletta and Mickey want."

"Who's Mickey?" Reese snagged a spoon from the drawer and mixed the chocolate five times over.

"Her..." Creed wrinkled his nose.

"Partner." I prompted him as I eyed Reese and tried to figure out how soon I could get my hands on my favorite drink.

"And they're a director." Malik put the saucepan back on the stove, choosing a cold burner. "They directed the Grindstone documentary."

"Oh wow. That's so cool. You heard Axel wound up getting together with his teacher, right? How he sang a song to the guy at Rocktoberfest and now they're a couple?" Freddie sauntered over to snag a mug—clearly having forgotten whatever he'd planned to grab from the fridge.

"They're going to be here in just a few minutes." I grabbed my mug. "We need to decide where we're going to sit."

"Is this, like, a formal thing?" Reese put the spoon in the sink and swiped her mug.

"She said she's bringing a contract for us to look over." Malik shrugged. "She didn't give specifics."

"I made it clear no one is signing anything tonight." I met each of their gazes. "Your entertainment lawyer is one of the best in Vancouver—so you're going to listen to her."

Creed rolled his eyes.

Malik swatted him. "This is serious."

"Hey, I am serious." Creed appeared vaguely wounded with a furrowed brow.

"Is she offering a representation deal?"

I nodded. "That was my understanding. And something about an executive producer."

"She was a little cagey about that. *Award-winning*." Malik used air quotes.

"Ah." Even as Reese said the word, she jolted when the doorbell rang.

"I'll get it." Malik headed for the front door. Just before he was out of sight, though, he met my gaze. "Family room."

I nodded. After he left, I turned to the assembled group. "How about you make yourselves at home? Malik and I can prepare the drinks."

Creed locked arms with Reese and gestured to Freddie with his chin.

The three headed toward the far side of this cavernous room that stretched the length of the back of the house.

I'd always thought the space large and imposing.

With the three of them chatting excitedly—albeit quietly—the place felt less imposing. This house was meant for lots of people. I could imagine how it had been with just Malik and his parents. Equally able to swallow up just Malik and myself. Add the band, though, and now these two strangers? The place felt more alive than it had in the entire time I'd been staying here.

And he just asked me to move in. That had to mean something. Tonight? Of all nights? The winter solstice was an incredibly important day for Indigenous people. I wasn't one, of course, but this had always been Pike's favorite day of the year.

"This is the family room slash kitchen." Malik guided two people into the room.

One was slightly shorter with brown curly hair and curious eyes. Likely Mickey, although I'd never seen them in person.

The other was a stunning Black woman who was nearly Malik's height. Pauletta Magnum commanded presence on television—she was even more stunning in person.

"We have hot chocolate, tea, cola, water..." Malik met my gaze with a touch of desperation.

I grinned, pulling from my years of experience of making people feel at home. "Hot chocolate is still quite hot, and everything else will take mere moments to make."

Pauletta linked arms with her partner. "We both love hot chocolate and rarely have it."

"Two mugs coming up. Marshmallows or plain?"

Mickey's eyes lit.

Pauletta laughed.

"With marshmallows coming up." I hadn't given it to the others—an oversight—but they could ask if they really wanted, and clearly they hadn't. Or had been too nervous to think about it.

The three people moved my way, and I organized the drinks.

Mickey and Pauletta followed Malik toward the family room while I ensured the kitchen was more or less put to rights. After a moment, I joined the group, taking the seat next to Malik. The space held two long couches and four comfortable chairs. Reese, Freddie, and Creed occupied one couch, Malik and I the other.

Our guests sat in chairs next to each other that had been moved closer together. While Mickey sipped their hot chocolate, Pauletta whipped out the contracts. She passed them around.

Everyone except Mickey put their hot chocolates on the coffee table and sat back. Only Malik and I actually started to read the contract.

Freddie waved his copy. "Can you topline this? Spencer says our lawyer needs to look over everything anyway."

Pauletta cocked her head at me. "Are you their rep?"

"Just a boyfriend and concerned party."

"You're a far way from corporate law. Or environmental legislation."

Ah. You've done your homework. Well done. Not that I expected any less—any rep worth their salt would walk in prepared. "And you've only ever repped Grindstone. Yet here you are."

"I spoke to them before coming here. They'll always be my first clients—and I'm forever grateful—but I am capable of being attentive to more than one band."

"Your loyalties will always lie with them."

She cocked her head. "I will ensure you never come into conflict with them."

"I believe they're competing for a spot at Rocktoberfest."

"They've gone the last two years without incident. No reason they won't return if they want to."

Malik shot me a glance before focusing on Pauletta. "Why would they not want to?"

"Meg, their drummer, just had a baby. She and Big Mac will have their hands full."

Big Mac was also a member of the band.

"Don't they have a tour before then?"

"A smaller one, yes. Culminating in a performance at Massey Hall in Toronto."

"Rocktoberfest is just one performance." I pressed my knee to Malik.

"That's true. I believe if they want a spot, it's theirs. Several other bands won't be attending, however. Also, they've opened up more slots since the event continues to grow in size." Pauletta held my gaze.

"You think we have a shot?" Creed had rolled his contract into a cone. Like a child would so they could shout through it in an attempt to make themselves sound louder. Naturally, I hoped he didn't plan to do that tonight. He always was the wild card in this group.

"I do." Pauletta's gaze traveled from every member of the band, but lingered on Malik.

Interesting. Does she realize he sort of leads this ragtag group? Likely.

"There's a but." Malik again pressed his knee to mine. "There's always a but."

"Carson Keriakos."

Hell, even I knew the name. I might not have inhaled sharply—like every member of the band did—but I was damn curious.

"What about Carson Keriakos?" Reese scanned the contract with intense interest, her brow furrowing.

Creed dropped his to the table and picked up his hot chocolate. "Before it gets cold." He took a sip.

I scanned the contract, specifically looking for the name.

Pauletta put her briefcase next to her chair and picked up her mug as well, taking a sip. "Mr. Keriakos is offering to produce your next album."

Creed pumped his first in the air.

Reese managed to rescue the hot chocolate he nearly tipped—by dropping her copy of the contract.

"Uh, sorry." Creed didn't appear to be the least bit repentant.

Malik had assured me, quite some time ago, that they had every cleaning product known to man, and if for some reason he couldn't get a stain out, his cleaner likely could.

I was still grateful to Reese.

"What's the catch?" I placed the contract on my lap and snagged my hot chocolate. I knew, of course. Had absorbed enough through my scan of the contract.

"It's not really a catch—" Pauletta cut herself off, clearly having spotted my arched eyebrow. "He's asking for seven months."

Freddie whistled.

Reese blinked.

Creed fist pumped again.

Malik inhaled sharply.

"Seven months is a long time. That would be the beginning of January until the end of July. I don't know much about music, but I don't believe it takes seven months to produce an album." I wanted to ensure we were all on the same page.

Pauletta pursed her lips. "Perhaps not. What Carson is offering is more than an album, though. He's offering to create a cohesive band. To up their game. To help secure them a spot in the Rocktoberfest lineup."

"Seven months is still a long time. They have lives here in Vancouver."

Malik shot me a look.

I shrugged. "You're expected to stay secluded on his Greek island for the entire seven months."

Reese's eyes went wide. "Are you shitting me?"

I shook my head. "It's all spelled out in the contract. Now, I didn't catch all of the details—and I don't know how much is negotiable."

"Not much." Pauletta sipped her hot chocolate again. "This is damn good."

"Uh, thanks." Malik continued to flip pages. "Seven months?" He cast me a surreptitious glance.

Don't give anything away. You'll miss him like fuck, but this could be his big break. "I think they need some time—"

"I don't." Creed raised his mug. "Carson Keriakos? Tell me where and when and I'm there. He's just about the best there is."

"He's..." Malik gestured.

"Eccentric?" Reese contributing.

"Filthy rich?" Freddie having his say.

"Award-winning." Malik placed his contract on the coffee table and took his mug. He didn't lean back. "You've given us a lot to consider. Is your offer of representation contingent on whether we accept or not?"

Pauletta held his gaze. "One is negotiable. One is not."

Her answer felt cryptic to me, but Malik nodded. "Understood."

Mickey raised their hand.

Absurdly, I nodded.

"Mr. Keriakos has invited me to shoot a documentary about your time on the island. Well, I'd be the director. Lydia is the videographer, Kato is the sound engineer, and Thornton Graves would be doing much of the interviews. None of us would be there full-time, though. We'd come in periodically."

"That's the same with me." Pauletta wrapped her hands around her mug. "I would have regular check-ins with all of you—to ensure everything's running smoothly."

"What about our family?" Freddie tapped the contract.

"You'll have weekly phone calls, and for a week in May, they might visit."

"That's it?" Reese frowned. "This seems..." She gestured.

"Controlling?" I met Pauletta's gaze.

"He has a process." She looked at each band member. "He's award-winning for a reason. I think a couple of years ago, Grindstone would've done anything for this opportunity. That you're receiving it so early in your career shows Carson thinks highly of you. He sees great potential."

"And he won't consider coming to Vancouver? Or maybe a studio in London or LA?" I didn't have authorization to negotiate on behalf of the band. That said, I wanted to know what other options were open.

Pauletta shook her head. "This is an all-or-nothing deal. They go to Greece or they're on their own."

"That's pretty harsh."

She arched an eyebrow at me. "I can still rep them, but they'd be fools to give this up."

"Maybe we have reasons for wanting to stay in Vancouver—"

"Malik." I said his name quietly.

"I'm in." Creed puffed up his chest. "Mama will be thrilled to get rid of me for seven months."

I wasn't so certain. Mama Murthi carried on about wanting her son to *grow up and move out*, but she also gave him every incentive to stay—including home-cooked meals, laundry, and very little hassle.

"My employer." Reese ran a hand through her hair. "We'll be past Christmas and New Year, right? We leave on January fourth?"

"Yes, that's correct." Pauletta sat a little straighter—as if she could see she was on the verge of winning this battle.

"I have a life in Vancouver." Malik again pressed his knee against mine.

"We can talk about it later." I met his gaze as it shot to mine. "Or Moses and I move in here to take care of your place."

"Our place. I already asked you to move in."

"Woo-hoo." Creed put his mug down, rose, and did a weird little happy dance.

"Aw shit." Reese opened her phone case and produced the twenty-dollar bill she always kept hidden.

Freddie yanked his wallet from his back pocket and handed over a twenty as well with a rather disgruntled look on his face. "Thank God I didn't agree to the hundred you wanted." He shot a glare my way. "You couldn't have waited until the new year?"

Reese sighed. "Or Valentine's Day?"

"I haven't moved in yet." Truthfully, I found this amusing.

"But he asked, right?" Reese regarded me.

I didn't consider lying. "Yeah, just now. When did you three place the wager?"

"Halloween. His idea." She gestured to Creed. "I knew I was running a risk, but I honestly thought Malik had more sense." She winced. "Not about you. This has very little to do with you."

Malik chuckled. "Oh, I'd say it has everything to do with Spencer. And, for the record, I would've asked around Halloween if I could've gotten him to agree. He likes to take his time. He eases into things."

"Greece is a great opportunity." I held his gaze. "Moses and I will cope in this big place." I intended to keep to a small portion of the place as my cat having free rein to roam didn't feel like a good idea.

Slowly, he nodded.

"They have to have a private sit-down. They need to speak to their lawyer." I aimed my best lawyerly stare at Pauletta.

She grinned. "Wouldn't have it any other way. We'd appreciate a response before Christmas. Carson will send his private jet on the fourth."

"Jesus." Freddie whispered that.

I'd never flown more than business class on a 747. I was impressed. I shouldn't have been...but I was. I hoped this display of wealth didn't sway the others.

Reese rose. "I have to get going." She eyed me. "You'll set up a meeting with our lawyer? You have my availability."

Being left to the task didn't bother me. That she trusted me to organize things was a bit of an honor. She was often the brains of the group. "Of course. Happy to."

"Right." She headed out of the room.

"I'll see her out." Malik rose.

Freddie gestured for him to sit back down. "Creed and I are just leaving."

"We are?" Creed's eyebrows shot up.

"We are." Freddie smacked his biceps.

Creed rose, and the two headed out.

Pauletta was slower to rise. "Anything I can say to convince you?" She directed the question at Malik, but her gaze flitted to me for just a moment.

She knows how to read the room.

"We'll be in touch." I rose. "Nice to meet you both."

Mickey bounced out of their chair. "I hope you say *yes*. Not just because I'd love the opportunity to hang out on a private Greek island, though." They met Malik's gaze. "Because Pauletta believes in you. That means something. Okay, bye." They bounded out—almost like a puppy.

Pauletta laughed. "They're not always so enthusiastic. They're not wrong either."

"You make a lovely couple." I didn't normally comment on personal things, but Pauletta appeared besotted.

"More than a year and still going strong. We met because of Grindstone." She turned to me. "They'll always have an important part of my heart—but when it comes to business, I'm easily able to split my focus. I'll do right by Razor Made. I promise."

I believed her.

Chapter Twenty-Two

Malik

"It's snowing." I gazed through the slats of my blinds. Usually I closed them when bedtime came, but I'd had the feeling snow was coming, and I loved nothing more than to lie in bed, in the dark, and to watch the snow swirling around the streetlamp. We didn't get much snow in the Lower Mainland. A few days a year. Snow days when school was canceled were even rarer.

Spencer, who lay on the far side of the bed, away from the window, propped himself up on his elbow so he could see over me. "Yeah, that's so cool. I hope I don't have a problem getting home to Moses in the morning."

"Or to the lawyer's office." I tried to keep my tone neutral.

"You're worried."

I shrugged nonchalantly—even though my gut churned. "We'll see what she has to say. Pauletta sent her a digital copy tonight, and she emailed me that she received it. I sort of feel guilty that she's looking it over tonight—"

"You pay her a lot of money."

I chuckled. "Yeah, we do. She's worth every penny. She's a shark. Unlike you."

"I don't know how to take that statement."

"You're a teddy bear."

He pressed his body against mine. His cock, although flaccid, pressed against my hip. *How difficult would it be to arouse him again?* We'd already gone at it twice tonight. I wasn't sated. I was never sated when it came to Spencer.

And that scared me just a little bit.

"Reese's message came through after you fell asleep." I gazed over at him, tearing my eyes away from the falling snow. "That's five for five. *If* the lawyer approves."

Slowly, he nodded. "She might make some suggestions, but Pauletta made it clear very little was negotiable. I've never heard of a band hiding away for seven months."

"We're a rock band—we do weird shit. Carson...he's the best there is."

"Interestingly, Pauletta never clarified whether she sought him out or he sought her out."

"You mean why he didn't just present us the offer himself?"

"Yeah."

I grinned. "The guy's related to Kato—Mickey's sound engineer. Distant relative but..." I shrugged. Life was all about people who knew people. If not for some guy I'd never met, this opportunity might never have landed in my lap.

"So you figure Carson made the offer through Pauletta because he knew her?"

"Or knew of her. I think—" I drew in a breath. "I think he chose us. Rather than her suggesting us. I have no idea how we'd even be on the guy's radar."

"Probably has a lot of fingers in a lot of pies. Razor Made has had a couple of videos go viral. And you're not known as rabble rousers."

"Except when we chain ourselves to bridges."

He chuckled. "Yeah. That." His expression sobered.

"What?" I shifted so I lay on my side, facing him. The snow would likely still be there in the morning. Not with the same weird neon-pink glow to it, but beautiful nonetheless.

"I'm thinking about Pike."

I blinked. "The fish? You're thinking about fish *now*? I don't think we have any—although I could check the freezer." I wracked my brain. I wasn't a huge fish fan.

He smiled, pressing a thumb to my frown line. "Relax. I didn't mean the fish. I mean Pike was named for a fish, but he wasn't a fish."

"But he was a man."

"He was."

Curiosity ate away at me, but I'd learned sometimes Spencer needed time to process things. I could word vomit just about anything. Well, except stuff to do with my parents and that loss. Those thoughts came slower. Were harder to express.

"He died two years ago." He blinked several times. I could barely see the green of his irises in the darkness of the room. Still, that little bit of the light filtered in from the streetlamp.

"You've never mentioned him."

Spencer closed his eyes for a moment. Then he pressed his fingers against his closed lids. "I try not to think about him. Because it's too goddamned painful."

Quietly, I placed my hand on her sternum. He always carried his tension there. I pressed. "You don't have to."

He pulled his fingers away from his eyes and his lids fluttered open.

A lone tear escaped. It ran across the bridge of his nose and fell without a sound to the pillow beneath his head. Another one formed and, on impulse, I leaned over to kiss it away.

He wrapped his arm around me.

I did the same, pulling him close.

He wept.

Time had no meaning in moments like this. I was close to the seven-year anniversary of my parents' death. I'd still been so damn raw at two years. Still walking around in a daze—unable to comprehend I was now truly alone in the world. Only Charles, and the other members of the symphony, had gotten me through those rough years.

And who did Spencer have? Certainly not his parents. Two years ago? He hadn't been working at TLIO at that point. Or had he? *I should've paid more attention. I should've asked more questions. I should've been more considerate to him and his needs.* Being a selfish prick sometimes came more easily than I would've liked. On occasion, I had to remind myself the world didn't revolve around me.

Spencer helped with that.

Eventually his weeping eased.

He sniffled.

I reached over to my bedside, snagged a tissue, and handed it to him.

He blew his nose. A loud, honking sound.

Despite the strong desire to, I managed not to laugh. Barely.

"Sorry." He held the tissue in his hand.

I grabbed the only unsoiled edge and flung it over the bed. *I'll deal with it in the morning...or maybe convince him to do it.* Regardless,

I'd have it picked up before the cleaner arrived. "You don't need to apologize."

"But I feel like I do. You didn't sign up for a weepy guy."

"That's true. I didn't sign up for any guy. Let alone a handsome, charming, sexy one with the most adorable cat ever."

"You're lucky he likes you."

"I consider myself honored." I tucked him against my shoulder. "Can you talk about it? Or do you just want to rest?"

"It's been two years. That's a long time."

"Or it passes in the blink of an eye. I was just thinking I lost my parents almost seven years ago. Sometimes I forget what their voices sounded like. I have a few videos I could get out and watch...but that feels morbid. Time is supposed to heal. If I keep ripping off the bandage, it never will."

"That's true." He sniffed. "Pike was my best friend when we were growing up. We both lived in virtual poverty—although his was more the system while mine was my parents eschewing all things material."

I understood *eschewing*. I didn't understand *the system*.

"He was Indigenous."

"Ah." Then little doubt that systemic racism played a part. All the wealth in the world didn't change the fact I was Black. I'd been raised to be proud of that—but I witnessed racism of all stripes. "You remained friends?"

"Yeah. Eventually he got tired of living a crappy life in the city and he went back to his reserve in the interior. He used his knowledge to fight within the system for a better life for his family and friends. I don't know where he found the strength."

"You were what, going to law school?"

"Living in a comfortable dorm and eventually a comfortable condo and earning lots of money, yeah. He was working as a social worker in his community. That's—" He swallowed.

"Social work is tough just about everywhere. Takes a special kind of person to do that work."

"Yep. That was Pike. He was special...and I didn't pay enough attention."

My senses went on high alert at his tone as much as his words.

"What happened?"

"The government decided to build a pipeline right through his territory. He didn't take kindly to that."

"Ah." A picture was slowly coalescing in my mind.

"The promised jobs were enough to sway some in his tribe. Others saw only the destruction of pristine wilderness and the decimation should the pipeline rupture."

"What was Pike's view?"

Spencer worked his lower lip through his teeth. "Adamantly opposed. Sure, the money would've been great, but he didn't see the upside. He had truly left the city behind and was steeped in the land. The wilderness had taken on an almost mystical quality to him. He wrote of it often. As much as he was tired of the poverty and substance abuse, he believed he could help lead people to a better life. He was talking about ecotourism. And the government was doing huge ad campaigns encouraging Indigenous tourism. He saw that as a better source of revenue. He—" Spencer hiccupped. "He fought big oil. He fought the government. He...lost."

I couldn't quite piece things together.

"They set up a barricade to prevent the pipeline. The courts ordered them to dismantle the camp. They didn't. The cops arrived—" He shut his eyes. "I saw it on the news. The fucking news. Two days after

I'd turned in my company to the authorities. Authorities I trusted. And yeah, the cops investigating the fraud where I worked obviously weren't the same cops up north..."

"But it felt like the system all over again." This, I could understand.

"Yeah." He wiped at his face. "The pipeline will be finished in the spring and operational by summer. He never stood a chance."

"He's the reason you fight."

"Sure." He sighed. "I wasn't there for him. When I left the company, I reread all his emails to me. I didn't see the desperation in them. Beneath the upbeat updates was a desperation I could only see after the fact. When everything sort of worked itself out. When the pieces fell into place."

"What happened to the cops?"

"They claimed self-defense. I was hoping there might be an inquiry, but nothing's happened yet. The band got their money. Someone is trying to organize a scholarship in Pike's name. I've contributed, of course."

"Of course." I echoed the words. Given how little he actually made, that would've been a sacrifice. "And you came to work for This Land is Ours."

"Yep. Full circle. Back to where my parents started forty years ago."

"But you have a chance. You know how the system works."

"Not really. I don't have connections to the back rooms. I can't influence politicians and policy makers. I'm adept at reading documents and finding flaws, but what good is that really?"

I didn't know. I honestly didn't know. "You still fight for the disadvantaged. That night, at city council—" *The night you almost fucked everything up.*

He chuckled. "Not one of my better nights."

"I'm sorry—"

"You don't need to be. Your passion far exceeded mine. I hoped I could apply logic and reason. You showed them people cared. Understood what was at stake." He sniffed.

"Where do you go from here?"

"I don't know. I took the job with the hope of somehow making a difference. Of honoring Pike's legacy. I'm not sure I'm succeeding."

"You take on a lot of battles."

"Yep. Indigenous rights. The environment. Poverty. Systemic racism. I'm trying to fight on so many fronts, and making little headway with any of them."

And working yourself to the bone. Something had to give. I just didn't know what. Before I could say anything, though, he kept speaking.

"Winter solstice was his favorite time of year. Followed by summer solstice. That last winter, he invited me up to join him. I—" He swallowed. "I had a major project due at the beginning of the year and I put him off. Within a couple of months, he'd died, and I'd turned whistleblower. I didn't even go up for his funeral. Honestly, I wasn't certain I'd be welcome."

That hurt my heart. "And you remember him on each solstice?"

"Yeah. Last year I trekked up to the Arctic circle for the summer solstice. Longest day of the year. Night was barely a blink. No way would I go up in the dead of winter, though. I like my daylight, thank you very much."

"You just don't want your cock to freeze and fall off."

He chuckled. "Yeah, that too."

"Would you want to go? To where he died? To where he lived?"

"I don't think so. I keep him in my heart. I honor his memory by doing whatever I can to advance the causes he believed in. Doing more would be better..."

"But you're only one person, and you only have so many hours in the day."

"Yeah, something like that."

I knew when he used *yeah* that he was getting tired. "Will you let me hold you?"

"Yeah. I'd really like that."

"Turn over. Scooch back against me. Let me keep you close. Let me keep you safe." I wouldn't always be here, of course. A private island off of Greece beckoned. But, for this one night, I could hold him close. I'd go to the lawyer's tomorrow and sign the paperwork. We'd move Spencer and Moses into the house. We'd celebrate Christmas.

Then, on the fourth of January, I'd board a private jet and head into an unknown world.

Frankly, I was fucking terrified.

Long after his breathing had evened, mine did as well.

Chapter Twenty-Three

Spencer

Whereas I'd thought Christmas would be a nice, quiet, private event with just Malik and myself, the reality turned out to be quite different.

Oh, we had a restful lie in—except that Moses got it into his head that he needed to be fed at six in the morning and decided kneading Malik's hair with his claws was the way to get his needs met.

Malik, the old softie, rose and fed the damn cat. He also insisted—insisted—that Moses have free run of the entire house. Now, he'd at least removed all the valuable and breakable things to his parents' room, and that space remained closed off.

Moses, never a fan of closed doors, would sit and yowl at it.

Seriously, my cat had a massive attitude problem.

Still, he'd already found a spot in Mrs. Forestal's study where he could bathe in sunlight and lick his paws to his heart's content.

I'd already taken the fur-remover thing to the area twice.

Having met the cleaner the day after the solstice, I apologized profusely and said I'd do my best to keep up with my cat.

The woman laughed, pointed out she didn't have enough to fill her time anyway, and assured me she was happy to do a little extra.

At that moment, Moses leapt onto the kitchen table and head-butted the woman's hand.

Turning on the charm. So like my finicky feline.

During our party on Christmas afternoon, however, he made himself scarce.

I would've too, if I'd known just how many people would be *dropping in*. Like, about half the symphony, all of Razor Made, a good portion of their families, and a few people from the neighborhood.

Malik contended he was alone in the world. A loner.

To the contrary, the dozens of people scattered about the house showed that to either be a lie or a fundamental misunderstanding on his part as to what *alone* meant. Because alone and lonely were two very different things.

Bonnie and Blossom also dropped in—along with several other of my coworkers who Malik had invited. He took seriously his role as my *partner* and always showed a keen interest in whatever I was working on.

As I shared an interest in his music. Pretty easy these days since he spent a lot of time in his studio. He was happiest, clearly, when I was close-at-hand. So, I'd take my laptop downstairs and work on the couch while he jammed with the band.

"You look happier than the first time we met." Mama Murthi planted herself before me across the kitchen island. I was preparing yet another tray of pigs in a blanket and tzatziki crusty thingies. Hell, I didn't even know their name.

"I try." Before I could escape to start passing them around, Pauletta breezed into the kitchen.

"Oh, perfect." She snagged the tray and headed right back out.

I met Mama's gaze.

She grinned. "I like that girl."

"I think she'd take issue with you referring to her as a *girl*."

Mama shrugged. "I've figured out that she's with a nonbinary partner. At my age, I can get away with a lot."

I arched an eyebrow as I checked the stove. "Who knew pigs in a blanket would be so popular?"

"I think Creed's eating all of them. I don't serve them in my house." Before I could ask, she said, "Unhealthy."

Knowing that pointing out all the other junk food she served would be tactless, I simply smiled. "Well, he's getting his fill today." I pulled a tray from the fridge.

The thing was covered in little piles of Ritz crackers with a cube of ham and a bit of cheese attached with a toothpick. Again, I would've expected...something more upscale? Fancier?

Malik had contemplated hiring a caterer.

I'd said I could manage. Of course, I'd thought we were talking about a dozen people at the most. Now I almost wish we had splurged for help. Not that I minded hanging out in the kitchen. Most of the guests had visited at some point or other to chat with me. I hadn't seen much of Malik, but I wasn't someone who was needy and required constant contact. As a lawyer, I met strangers all the time. Unless they were an adversary—and sometimes even then—I needed to make people at ease.

Now, however, I was alone with Mama.

So maybe not so much at ease.

Freddie appeared, eyed the tray of hors d'oeuvres, and his grin widened.

I held it out. "To share."

He eyed Mama Murthi. "Of course." He contemplated the tray and almost held it out.

She waved him off.

He scurried away.

I opened the fridge and pulled out a tray of vegetables. "Straight from Mexico." Cherry tomatoes, baby carrots, as well as slices of cauliflower and broccoli. This tray I'd bought from the store. I removed the plastic seal from the lid, then pushed the entire tray toward her.

"Do you have a fancier plate?"

"What, the plastic container isn't upscale enough?" I disappeared into the dining room and returned with a china plate with a pink rose pattern with gold trim. At least I knew this didn't go in the dishwasher.

Mama smiled. "Yes, I can see Mrs. Forestal using that."

I cocked my head. "You didn't know her, did you?"

She shook her head. She washed her hands, then with a fork, moved the vegetables to the serving platter—ensuring none of the vegetables mingled. "I did not. But Malik has spoken of her. He probably doesn't even realize how much he gives away."

"You're an easy person to talk to."

She pointed the fork at me. "You're a lawyer. You contemplate every word unless you're extremely excited or agitated."

I removed a tray of pre-cut fruit. "Be right back."

"I have your number, Spencer."

At her words, I smiled. Yes, she did. She really did. I never wanted to face her either at the boardroom table or in a courtroom. She'd likely wipe the floor with me.

I returned with another platter. This one had geometric patterns. I held it up.

"A gift from Reese after last year's party."

"Ah. So this truly is Malik's. I wondered."

"Smart woman. She spotted him with the floral and decided he needed something of his own."

I swapped the vegetable platter for the fruit tray and the geometric serving thing. Not quite a tray. Not quite a bowl. Hell, I had less experience with fancy things than most people here. I hadn't entertained much at my condo. And, of course, I hadn't used any of this while I was growing up.

Mama washed the fork, then set to work moving the fruit to the platter thingy.

I was about to wander out with the veggie tray when Malik entered holding the empty plate that had held the pigs in a blanket.

"Creed?" Mama arched her eyebrows.

"Nope. I kept him occupied while Freddie passed these around. Creed only got the last one."

I chuckled. "I bet he's irritated."

"Oh, you have no idea."

Mama pushed the veggie tray. "Healthy."

He grinned, pecked her on the cheek, grabbed the rose-patterned platter with the veggies, and headed out.

I put the precooked tray of apple crumble into the oven.

Mickey appeared. "Malik said you had a tray of fruit?" They were slightly hesitant.

Mama laughed. "Roped you in, did he?" She passed over the tray. "All ready to go. Spencer is working on the desserts."

"Well, I can do that." Mickey met my gaze. "You should be enjoying yourself."

"I am, trust me." I gestured to Mama. "Best company in the world."

Mickey smiled. "Yes, I can see that." They took the tray and headed back toward the guests.

"Nice person. Always quick with a smile."

"They're going to be filming a documentary." I eyed Mama. "If any of the band members have skeletons in their closet, Mickey will ferret them out."

Mama waved away my concern. "Nothing they can't handle."

I assumed when she said *they* that she meant the band members—including both her son and Malik. "I hope you're right."

I opened the fridge. "I got mini chocolate éclairs. I hope they didn't get soggy when I defrosted them."

"Well, I'll just have to check for you." Mama grinned wickedly.

"Of course." I handed her the bucket, tongs, and a plain kitchen plate. This was chocolate—no one was going to care what the delights were served from. "I also have mini-Nanaimo bars."

Mama licked her lips. "I'll have to taste test them as well. Finally, I will tell you a secret."

I stilled.

She waved me off. "Nothing like that. I spoke to Pauletta earlier—she's friends with Hugo Threadgold."

I cocked my head.

"He's dating Axel Townsend. Well, they're engaged."

"The lead singer from Grindstone? I didn't realize you have a connection to the band."

"Passing acquaintance. Renee. She's a teacher at a high-end private school. One of her kids was accused of a crime they didn't commit. Renee was an alibi, so to speak. I worked with her to convince the authorities they had the wrong person in custody. We keep in touch."

"That student was lucky they had not one but two people who cared."

Again, Mama waved me off.

I did wonder why a student who attended a high-end private school required a legal aid lawyer. Perhaps a scholarship student? None of my business, of course, but I was curious. "So you know Renee."

"Yes." Mama pointed to the éclairs. "Perfect." She sighed. "I almost wish they weren't so I could eat them all myself."

"I promise to always have some in the freezer for when you come to visit."

"Lovely." She finished arranging them on the plate. "I think I might distribute these myself. To keep Freddie from eating all of them at once."

"You're not worried about Creed or Malik?"

She snickered as she slid off the bar stool which had really been too high for her—but she'd managed. She always found a way to cope with everything life threw at her.

I admired her for that.

"Creed and Malike know better. Freddie will try."

I plated the Nanaimo bar bite-sized chunks. "Better send someone in."

"Done. Don't tell the band about Grindstone."

I frowned.

"Oh, Pauletta and Renee are organizing for them to meet with Razor Made before that crew heads to that private island." She snagged the plate of éclairs. "I did my research on that guy."

"Me too. Quirky."

She snickered again. "You can say that again. All right, young man." She held out the plate.

I snagged one, knowing full well there wouldn't be any left by the time she returned. "Thank you."

"No worries. I'll send someone in to grab the next tray."

I grabbed a bite-sized piece of Nanaimo bar and popped it into my mouth.

She winked, and then she was gone.

And just like that, I realized I felt a lot less lonely.

We're lucky to have her in our lives.

Malik, most especially. Mama couldn't make up for the loss of his parents—but she could be a calming influence on a man whose mind often raced. She could give him stability when he lacked grounding.

I hope I can be a good influence on him as well. That he'll turn to me if he needs comfort and support.

On that note, I grabbed another bite.

Creed sailed into the kitchen.

I handed him the plate.

He shoved a piece into his mouth, saluted, and headed out.

I chuckled to myself and then checked on the apple crumble.

Yeah. We're going to be okay.

I'd miss him like crazy. But we'd be okay.

Chapter Twenty-Four

Malik

"Stop fidgeting." Spencer took my hand in his. "I know this is a big deal. They're also just regular guys."

"They're freaking Grindstone."

"Again, they're just regular people. Perhaps extraordinary musicians—like you all are—but ordinary people like yourselves."

He squeezed my hand.

I squeezed back—twice as hard.

He winced.

I tried to let go.

He covered my hand with both of his.

We sat in my formal living room because this room was closer to the front door. We'd gone back and forth with Pauletta about the best place to meet the band. My place wound up being the most logical. Razor Made was comfortable here. Pauletta and Mickey had already visited.

Mickey, Kato, and Lydia were already set up in the family room where the official greeting was to take place. I wasn't certain about this all being recorded, but a long conversation with Mickey and Thornton Graves convinced me. Thornton was the executive producer while Mickey would be the director on this project. Kato and Lydia were thrilled to be heading to Greece.

This all overwhelmed.

A knock came at the door.

Pauletta.

She would've been able to see us through the front window and, more importantly, I might've told her how much the doorbell drove me nuts. I really needed to change it, but that was just one more thing on the list of things needing to be done.

Spencer released my hand, caught my gaze, then nodded. He rose and strode to the front door.

I followed behind. At a distance.

He'd moved in just before Christmas. Here we were, December thirtieth, and he'd already made himself at home. With my blessing, of course.

Moses was hanging out in my bedroom. We'd put a litter box for him in my ensuite bathroom, so he had everything he needed. When we didn't have guests, he wandered our house with perfect ease.

Our.

"Come on in." Spencer spoke clearly. "You're most welcome here. Why don't you put your coats in the front hall closet? Plenty of hangers."

"Appreciated." Pauletta's voice rang out—also clearly.

I moved toward the entryway to find all of Grindstone, as well as Pauletta, Thornton Graves, and Hugo Threadgold removing their coats. The snow from the twenty-first had continued for a while. We'd been almost snowed in. Residents of Cedar Valley and into the interior of the province had been hit far more than us. Melting had begun, but then the snow had returned yesterday with a vengeance, so I was grateful everyone was removing their boots as well.

Axel, the lead singer, was the first to hang up his coat and slip off his boots. He caught sight of me and grinned. "Man, this is so cool." He stepped forward with his hand extended.

I shook it. *I hope he doesn't feel how sweaty and clammy my hand is.*

Axel was the tallest of the bunch, followed by Thornton, Pauletta, and Hugo. Ed, the guitar player was shorter. Songbird, the keyboard player was next, followed by Meg, the drummer. Big Mac, the bassist, was the shortest of the bunch. He wrapped his arm protectively around Meg, who had the tiniest baby bump. The Indigenous woman was stunning and practically glowed. The color might've come from being out in the cold, or just that glow some pregnant women got.

Songbird was South Korean, while Pauletta, Axel, and Ed were Black. I was looking at a multicultural group and, frankly, that put me at ease. Just like having Creed in the band, with his Indian heritage, assisted a lot. I shouldn't feel that way—but I did.

Ed stepped forward next. "Thanks for hosting us. None of us has a place this elegant."

Thornton, his husband, came alongside him. "Ed and I are buying a new place in Vancouver. But we won't be closing on the place for a bit." His eyes shone. Amber? Whiskey? Truly unique, that was for certain.

After I'd shaken hands and introduced myself to the rest of the band, Spencer stepped forward. "Why don't we head into the family room. A bit cozier."

Axel grinned. "I hear you make a mean hot chocolate."

I was able to smile back. "I do. Pretty boring."

The singer linked arms with me. "I suspect you've got a decked-out kitchen."

Hugo laughed. "Unlike our tiny one."

Axel shrugged. "We're simple guys. A small kitchen suits us."

"Until they add kids." Songbird breezed past everyone and headed toward the direction Spencer had indicated.

Hugo started coughing.

Axel laughed. "Oh sweetheart, you so stepped into that one."

I assumed this had something to do with whether or not Axel and Hugo were going to have children.

"He loves his students. In a professional way," Axel was quick to clarify. "And I'm all over the place. ADHD and all that."

I wasn't certain whether or not someone who had ADHD should be a determining factor about having children, but I respected the fact he knew himself so well. He allowed me to guide us to the family room. "Do you want to come to the kitchen while I make the hot chocolate?"

"Once I've met Freddie, Reese, and Creed? You bet."

And so it went. Everyone shook everyone's hand. I encouraged Spencer to mingle with the group while Axel and I headed to the kitchen area. What I really hoped was my boyfriend might get a sense of what being engaged or married to a rock star entailed. Hugo and Thornton might be good for Spencer as the two men were clearly rooted in reality and not starry-eyed with their mates.

Just about everyone was willing to try my hot chocolate, so I poured enough to fill the saucepan.

"How are you handing things?" Axel retrieved fifteen mugs. That included enough for the film crew if they chose to take a break.

I eyed the saucepan and figured we'd need more. I grabbed a second pan and put that on another burner.

"Sorry, man. I'm making you do a lot of work." He slid onto a bar stool at the island.

"I don't mind. Making hot chocolate soothes me. Even if it's for a large group of people." I found two wooden spoons so I could stir. "What do you mean when you ask me how I'm handling things?" I was aware Lydia the videographer and Kato the sound engineer had slipped into the kitchen. Laughter filtered through from the family room on the other side of this massive space. In the fraction of a moment, I swore I caught Spencer's deep, resonant laugh.

"Well, heading to Europe."

I handed Axel the chocolate powder I used when making a large batch. Much as I would've loved to melt Swiss chocolate, I didn't have the time or patience for that tonight. "Did I plan on heading out of the country in the new year and being away for more than seven months?" I chuckled. "That would be a *no*. Would I be crazy to pass up the opportunity? That would be a *yes*. Sometimes you just have to go with the flow. I'm going to miss my home—"

"And Spencer."

"—and Spencer." I met his gaze. "But he's fully supportive. He wouldn't be the man I loved if he wasn't. I guess we'll find out if the adage *absence makes the heart grow fonder* is actually true or not." I continued to stir the milk.

"We're going on tour. Thornton has a documentary he's working on, and Hugo has his teaching. Ed and I are going to be without our significant others for a bit."

I cocked my head—indicating I was listening without speaking. Because, frankly, I wasn't certain what the correct response would be.

"You'll be without Spencer. And you're just beginning your relationship. I have that correct, right?"

I didn't ask how he knew. "Yeah, we met when I chained myself to the Lion's Gate Bridge."

"Which was pretty badassed."

"Which could have gotten me charged and barred from entering the US."

"Oh shit." Axel's face distorted in panic—as if he hadn't thought of that before.

"Right. Arrested and charged would mean no Rocktoberfest."

"Ouch. You've submitted a demo, right? An audition tape?"

I nodded. "We'll follow it up with something we record at Keriakos Studios. I don't know if the organizers will be willing to take a chance on a newbie band."

"We were new." Axel winked.

"A ten-year overnight success." I chuckled. The milk was boiling, so I turned down the heat.

Axel brought me the mugs one-by-one, and I poured the hot milk into them. Then he stirred each one.

"Grab the whipped cream from the fridge?" I'd finished pouring the milk—with just a smidge left—and I grabbed the marshmallows.

"Whipped cream *and* marshmallows?" Axel's eyes widened.

I chuckled. "However you would like."

"Yo, folks!" He turned toward the family room. "Hot chocolate! With whipped cream *and* marshmallows."

Hugo was the first to arrive. He shook his head as Axel filled his mug to the brim with the whipped cream. "All that extra sugar."

Axel swiped his index finger in the whipped cream and appeared to be aiming for Hugo's nose.

The man deftly caught it. "No, thanks." He sucked the whipped cream off Axel's finger.

The rock star gave him this dreamy smile.

Spencer started handing everyone their mugs.

Whereas I thought we might go back into the family room—where we'd be way more comfortable—we didn't. Meg, with Big Mac's assistance, slid onto a stool. Reese took one, Freddie a third, and Songbird the final one. We stood around, after having doctored our drinks and just...shot the shit.

About an hour later, after we'd exhausted tons of topics, everyone headed out. Lydia, Kato, and Mickey were the last to leave since they had to take down all the equipment. Funny how I'd forgotten they were there. I hadn't thought I would but, in the end, I was too wrapped up in all the anecdotes and advice Grindstone had to offer.

Spencer kissed my temple after I'd locked the front door.

I sagged against him. "How did I survive that?"

"With great ease. And hey, Pauletta helped us with the cleanup while the crew put their equipment away, so we can head right to bed."

"I gotta piss first. Two hot chocolates? That's enough caffeine to keep me wired."

"At least you didn't add half a can of whipped cream. Hugo said something about Axel bouncing off the walls." Spencer took my hand, shut off the lights, and guided me up the grand staircase.

"I wondered about a student getting together with his teacher. The fact there was nothing between them back then, and ten years have passed...that's reassuring, right?"

"Yep." He directed me toward my bedroom. "I'll clean up in the spare bathroom and meet you in bed."

My bathroom only had one sink, and although I didn't mind intimate quarters, Spencer still liked a bit of privacy—probably a hangover from the years of living in a one-bedroom apartment with his parents. He valued space. It didn't always have to be physical, although sometimes it was. Most of the time, he needed room to breathe. To think. I was happy to give him that space.

Fifteen minutes later, we were cuddled in bed.

I'd gently coaxed Moses into his covered cat bed.

He'd leapt out, darted through my open bedroom door, and headed out to do God knew what. I didn't have mice, so I wasn't too concerned about what mischief he might get up to. He seemed like a pretty smart guy, and I'd lay good money he'd be curled around our heads come morning.

"You really don't mind having a cat? He's a handful."

"I've often thought about getting a dog. Might not be fair to them though, you know? What with me touring."

"There are dog babysitters. Heck, you've now got me."

But for how long? He'd rented his condo to a UBC student for the winter semester. Since I was going to be in Greece, and he was here, it only made sense to have someone in his place. He'd met her through TLIO, so he trusted her. This way, he didn't have to go back and forth between the two places. He could settle in here and hopefully, be comfortable.

He pressed his erection against my ass.

I wriggled backward.

He groaned. "You're not too tired?"

"To fuck you? Oh, hell no."

"Fair enough."

We always slept in the buff. We'd also both been tested and had ditched the condoms as well.

He nuzzled my neck.

I reached behind to grasp his thigh. "How do you want it?"

"Me on my back. I want to see your face."

"Well, conveniently that happens to be my favorite position as well." He pressed a kiss to my shoulder blade, then rolled onto his back. He stretched to grab the bottle of lube—which he always kept at hand. He was a horny guy.

Oh, who the fuck was I kidding? I was just as randy. Anytime. Anywhere. He had only to crook his finger, and I'd grow hard with wanting him. We'd christened a few pieces of furniture in the house—always being careful about cum stains, of course. But he was helping me feel less like I was living here on someone else's good graces, and more like this was my home. It had been, for my entire life, but for the first time I felt comfortable in the space.

Moses and Spencer made the place more of a home and less of a showpiece.

I rolled over and found my lover preparing himself. Sometimes he was okay with me doing this part. When he was in a hurry, he'd just do the prep. I smiled as he spread his legs and handed me the lube.

After coating myself, I took a position between his legs.

He nodded.

I pressed in.

He breathed through the discomfort as he continued to hold my gaze.

"Hard and fast, okay? I'm ready to blow."

I grinned. "Blow away. I'm still going to fuck you through it." Nothing I loved more than for him to come first and for me to coax him through the orgasm as I sought my own.

Still, as I teetered on the edge, giving in came easily. I pounded into him, thrusting over and over again. His gaze never left mine as he pulled his lower lip through his teeth.

"Come on, Spencer, baby, give in. Go over, okay? I've got you." On those words I snapped my hips and buried myself as deeply as I could into him.

With a cry, he came.

Cum spurted out from his cock, hitting both our chests.

Damn, without even being touched. Pretty impressive. He always put everything he had into our lovemaking and, as I tumbled over the edge with him, I soared high above. I took in the two of us, clinging together, and hoped it would always be like this. That he'd never let me go. That I'd be with him, by his side, forever.

Chapter Twenty-Five

Spencer

"You need to stop moping." Mama Murthi swatted at Moses who'd decided to leap onto the kitchen island and try to nab some of her crab dip.

With a yowl, he scampered away.

"Sorry. He knows better."

She pointed the serving spoon at me. "You do as well, my young friend. They're back in about an hour."

"He wouldn't let me pick him up at the airport."

"Because a fancy limousine is driving him here." She continued stirring the dip as I tore up slices of pumpernickel to dip in it. "They're all coming here, my little one. That tells you something. They could have all gone to their respective homes, but they've chosen to come here. And they asked the two of us to be here. No one else."

"That doesn't strike you as odd?"

"He's not going to dump you in front of a roomful of people. He's not going to dump you at all. Here." She put a fork into the mix and apportioned enough for me to try.

My eyes closed as I moaned in bliss. "You know, I think your cooking is how I survived this."

"Ha!" She grinned. "Papa loves you almost as much as I do. I'm glad you stopped turning down my requests for visits and started honoring your elders."

I snickered. "You're not *that* much older than me."

She rolled her eyes. "You're closer in age to Malik than to me."

"Not by much."

"Pfft." She pointed to the bread. "Finish with that."

"Yes, Mama."

The first couple weeks after the band left, I moped around the house. Aside from work, I had nothing to occupy my time. Mama kept inviting me over. I kept making excuses. I wanted to feel sorry for myself. I'd finally met the man of my dreams—the love of my life—and he'd abandoned me.

Which was total bullshit.

He'd been presented with the opportunity of a lifetime and had left me installed in his mansion with everything my heart might desire, to pursue his lifelong dream.

I didn't have the right to feel sorry for myself.

Which Mama reiterated in spades the Saturday she arrived on my doorstep, battered down the barricades—imaginary, not real—and demanded admittance.

We'd become fast friends. And every Friday night from that week on, I was expected at the Murthi household for dinner.

Abrianna commented, about three months into the arrangement, that she saw more of me than she usually saw of Creed—and he lived there.

I'd wondered if I was supposed to be offended, but she quickly clarified that she *liked* having me around—much better mannered than her brother. Also, she considered me a better conversationalist. Okay, I took that compliment with grace.

The Murthis were more like my parents than my own were by the end of the seven months. Never was I more grateful for people—both that they had invited me in, but also that Malik had them in his life. That even if something happened, and I wasn't around anymore, that he'd be cared for.

"Stop moping!" Mama barked in a voice she rarely used.

"Sorry." I met her gaze.

"He still wants you. Every other week he asks if you're still living here. If you're still happy. If you still want him."

I frowned. "I tell him those things all the time." Well, when communication was permitted. This Keriakos dude might be a fantastic producer, but he was also a little on the quirky side. Everything was strictly controlled for the band. When they could call, when they could write, when they could hear from us.

Pauletta regularly assured me things were going well. She refused to share the footage Lydia shot, but promised it was *good shit*.

Whatever that meant.

"You, my child, need to let go of some of your vigilance. Did they not text fifteen minutes ago to say they'd landed?"

"Well...yes."

"Did they not say they had to taxi the plane to the airport, disembark, and go through customs?"

I rolled my eyes.

"Hey!"

My gaze snapped to Mama's.

She wagged her finger at me.

Shame heated my cheeks. "Yes, Mama, they said all that."

"And did they not say the limo is there waiting for them?"

"Yes...?"

"So what are you fussing about? The roast chicken is almost cooked. You have hamburgers and hot dogs for the grill. Heck, you even ensured the gas was set up to flow to the grill—even though it has never let you down before."

"The entire three times I've used it." I'd invited the Murthi clan over three times since spring had sprung, and each time they chose barbecue. My vegetable kebobs were a particular favorite.

"You worry too much." She pointed to the fridge.

I pulled out the plate of vegetable kebobs as well as the meat one. Then I handed her the marinade.

She got to work. Twenty minutes later, she hustled out to the barbecue to cook everything, even planning to start on the burgers and dogs.

I remained in the kitchen to watch over the chicken while mixing the salad dressing with the lettuce and croutons to make the Caesar salad. Then I pulled the plate of cut veggies from the fridge and added a container of dip to the platter as well. I restrained myself from checking the fridge for the tenth time to ensure I had everyone's favorite drink. Mama was right—I was going overboard.

Just...seven months was a fucking long time.

As the sound of the front door opening reached me, Malik's bellow of, "We're home," resonated.

I took a deep breath before I headed toward the front hallway.

He met me halfway.

For just an instant, we stared.

Then he threw himself into my arms.

I vaguely noted everyone else coming in, even as his lips pressed to mine.

The kiss was graphic, dirty, and everything I hoped for.

He grabbed my ass and hauled me against him. He pressed his erect cock against mine. He didn't even pull back when Mama Murthi tsked her disapproval.

"Hi, Mama." Creed's tone was part amusement, part relief. Even I could hear the love as he embraced his mother.

"Do I smell barbecue?" Freddie toed off his sandals and headed toward the kitchen.

Reese did the same.

Pauletta stepped into the house and immediately to the side so Lydia could film the reunion.

We agreed today would be informal shooting—nothing scripted or pre-planned.

So when Malik dropped to one knee, I couldn't have been more shocked.

He grasped my hand. "I wanted to propose before I left. I didn't want to tie you down, though. I wanted you to feel free to meet other men—"

"There's only ever been you." I wasn't going to mention Paul the asshole or the few other guys—what I felt for them paled in comparison. I could barely remember wanting to marry Paul and start a family with him. Thank Christ we never had.

Malik grinned. "Well, that's good. It's the same for me."

Since he'd dated more than I had, his words carried a larger impact. He'd sampled what was out there and had known he wanted to come home here. To me.

I knelt.

"Hey." He tried for indignation, but that totally fell flat as he continued to hold my hand, this time looking into my eyes. "I'm a bad bet."

"You're not."

"I get into all kinds of mischief."

"You won't."

Mama's snort had us turning toward the kitchen. All the band members, Mama, and Pauletta stood watching us.

Heat flooded my cheeks. I forced myself not to look at Lydia with her camera or Mickey who stood just behind her. "You just had to be public."

"Our relationship hasn't exactly been a secret."

"Hell, no." Creed—always having to stick his nose in it.

"I didn't want you to feel like you could say no."

I glared at Malik.

He shrugged. "Hedging my bets?"

"As if all those emails and letters weren't full of sap and goop. You know I want you. Have practically since the first time we met."

He chuckled.

As did Mama.

"Will you marry me?" He leaned closer. "Lydia has promised to destroy the video file if you say *no*."

As if. "Yes, I'll marry you. Sheesh, sometimes you can be a dumbass."

"For proposing in semi-public or for thinking you might turn me down?"

"Well, frankly, both." I took his cheeks in my hands and drew him in for a kiss.

"Give him the ring." Creed—ensuring he played a large part in this.

I pulled back from the embrace. "Ring?"

Malik shrugged. Then he dug into his pocket and pulled out a little ring box. "Will you marry me?" He shoved the box at me without opening it.

Curious, I slowly opened it. The ring appeared to be platinum. "Is that...?

"White gold." He pulled the ring out of the box. "With Celtic knots. I mean, I tried to think of something British. Or from my culture. I kept coming back to these because they're like...I dunno...infinity? Something that'll keep forever." He grasped my hand and slid the ring onto my right finger. "When we get married, I'm moving that to your left hand. I want everyone to know you're mine."

"And what about me?"

Freddie hooted. "Told ya he'd want one to give to you."

Malik winced.

Mama stepped up to us and handed me a box.

I cocked my head as I met her gaze.

She pointed toward her son.

I opened the ring box and gasped.

The ring was onyx black with the same raised Celtic pattern, only in sapphire blue. A truly unique piece of jewelry that totally matched Malik's personality. "How...?"

"My son has a big mouth. He found a picture on the internet of one similar to the one Malik bought for you and he hinted strongly you might appreciate my help."

Creed, in turn, hooted. "Now, can we eat?" Without waiting for a response, he headed toward the kitchen.

Good thing I'd turned the heat in the oven down—otherwise we'd be eating very rubbery chicken.

"Are your knees starting to hurt?" Malik caressed my cheek.

"Are you suggesting I'm getting old?"

He laughed. "Uh, no. I just think we should've knelt on a rug rather than the marble entryway."

"Agreed."

Together, leaning on each other, we rose.

"Where are your bags?"

"I asked the driver to put them in the garage—we'll sort everything out when people are willing to leave. Seeing as we last ate about eight hours ago, I'd say they're starving."

"Better believe it." Reese approached us.

She held out her arms for a hug.

I embraced her warmly. "You know?"

"We'd always known. From the moment the plane took off from Vancouver heading east, we knew. This guy took some time to come around to the idea, though."

I gazed at Malik.

He shrugged. "I didn't know if I was worthy of you. I had...a lot of time to figure myself out."

"Which definitely shows in the music. I can't wait to play it for you and Mama." Resse offered a genuine smile.

Malik grinned as well. "Wait until you hear the audition tape we sent to the Rocktoberfest organizers."

I stilled.

"Yeah, we kept that under wraps as well. We're in!" He threw his arms around me. "We're going to Black Rock in October."

I held him close to me, basking in his evident joy. "I love you."

"Yeah, me too." He chuckled. "I mean I love you too."

"It's okay to love yourself, you know."

He pulled back to meet my gaze. "Working on that."

Which was all I could ask for.

Chapter Twenty-Six

Malik

"Dude, I swear that goofy grin hasn't left your face in three months." Creed leaned over my bunk as I typed out a quick text to Spencer about our concert in Sacramento.

"If you meet someone as awesome as Spencer, you'll be goofy too." I waited for his reply, watching the bubbles. He always responded in complete sentences with proper punctuation. I ribbed him that it was an *old guy* thing.

He countered it was a *lawyer* thing. That he never wanted there to be any misunderstandings.

I didn't bother to point out that, without tone, words could always lead to misunderstandings.

—*I miss you too. Mama and I will meet you in Black Rock.* —

"There's that grin again."

I smacked his thigh. "You're just jealous because my fiancé is coming and you only have your mother. What happened to Seraphina?"

"She said monogamy wasn't in the cards if I was going to be out of the country for seven months."

"Ouch." I winced. "You never said anything."

"You were missing your very faithful man. Why was I going to yuck your yum?"

I frowned. "We're friends. That's sort of what friends are for."

"I told Reese."

"Oh." I squinted. "I don't know whether to be offended by that or not. I'm glad you talked to someone, though."

"Oh, don't kid yourself—she wasn't all that sympathetic. She never liked Seraphina. Always felt she was, like, a band bunny."

I chuckled. "For Razor Made? That's a bit of a stretch."

"Hey." He balanced himself as the bus hung a left turn.

The driver, Vera was a fantastic person. She used to fly Hercules planes into the arctic circle. After her military career, Pauletta's father had recruited her to work for him in various capacities.

Pauletta, being magnanimous, had convinced her father to front the costs of our tour. He'd done the same for Grindstone a few years back and had been rewarded handsomely for that investment. So, in the hopes of Razor Made making it big, Mr. Magnum was providing us with a tour bus. Our manager, the lovely Pauletta, had arranged six stops down the Pacific coast as we headed to Rocktoberfest. None of the stops would compare in size to Black Rock, but with every show we gained confidence. We got closer to the cohesion Carson spoke of so often. And we were able to test out the new songs.

The album, *Razor's Edge* was going to drop while we were on stage.

I didn't understand all the logistics involved with this. The music wouldn't be available to fans before the show, but they'd be able to download it afterward.

Carson swore this was the best way to do things. Too early, and the Rocktoberfest goers wouldn't get an exclusive. Too late and fans would be looking for something that didn't exist yet.

"Spencer's taking Mama to the airport? They're flying together?" Creed tapped a beat on his thigh.

"Yes, Spencer is taking Mama to the airport. Yes, Pauletta has organized a camper van for Mama. You're worrying way too much."

I was still trying to figure out when I'd get some quality time with my man. Quite possibly, that wasn't going to happen.

"I'm not worrying."

I arched an eyebrow.

"Well, you would be stressing if—" He winced. "Shit."

I patted his thigh. "Yes, if my mother was coming, I'd be worried about her."

"That was really insensitive of me."

"Dude." I used his favorite word. "She's been gone for years. She wouldn't want me wallowing in my grief."

"Yeah?" He cocked his head.

"Yeah." I sat up, careful not to hit my head.

He sat next to me. Close. Comfortingly.

"I'd do anything to have them back—but life doesn't work that way. Would they be happy knowing I'm on a tour bus and headed to a rock concert? Possibly not. Would they want *me* to be happy? Yes."

"But the symphony was to make them happy."

"True. I enjoyed it. Music's in my blood and my soul. Didn't get an ounce of that from my parents. In the end, though, as long as I'm performing, I'm happy. I'd like to believe they'd be pleased as well. We're dropping a record in just a couple of days."

"I still can't believe Carson chose us." He continued to drum his thigh.

"Neither can I." We'd never spoken about this because we hadn't wanted to jinx our good luck. To do anything to imperil our good fortune.

"Like, how did one of the biggest producers in the world hear about a little indie band from Vancouver?"

"And why did he pick us and ask us to give him nearly seven months?"

We eyed each other and, at the same time, said, "Pauletta."

I shook my head. "How did we not see this?"

"Partly because we didn't realize just how rich her father really is. He's one of the most successful business people in Vancouver—and that's saying something."

"So humoring her with a pet project would be a rounding error for him." I scratched my nose. "She must really believe in us."

"I think she does. And I'd be happy to ask her, but she isn't here." Our manager had the worst case of motion sickness. Tour buses were out, and airplanes required her to have heavy medication. If she drove herself, she was okay. She and Mickey were flying into Reno and then Pauletta was driving them to Black Rock.

Thornton, Lydia, and Kato had a camper van rented and were following our tour—joining us when they wanted to film things. Pretty chill.

Grindstone was in their own tour bus and were taking a direct route from Vancouver to Black Rock as they didn't have any concerts planned.

I eyed Thornton, who was playing a game of cards with Freddie. The poor guy was missing his husband terribly. Apparently the two men were planning for a big reunion once we all arrived at the campsite.

Axel was undoubtedly mooning over his husband, but Hugo hadn't been able to secure the time off school this year.

Which I thought was shitty, but Hugo said something about a professional commitment.

I'd keep an eye on Axel to make certain the guy wasn't too bummed out.

"Hey, we're just about there." Thornton waved. "And look at the bus ahead of us."

Creed vibrated next to me. "That's Maiden Fucking Voyage!"

Thornton cocked his head, with his slightly floppy blond hair going floppier.

"He means Maiden Voyage. We knew they were coming. Embrace the Fear, Social Sinners, Midnight Hunt, Queen Anne's Revenge, and Warrior Black are all going to be here as well." Excitement raced through me.

"Plus Grindstone." Thornton chuckled. "Please don't forget my husband's band."

"This is like a reunion for you, right?" I plopped myself on the bench seat next to him. "Any dirt you wish to dish?"

He shook his head. "You saw the documentary."

"Shit, man, I'm sorry." Thornton's younger sister had died from a drug overdose, and he'd blamed Axel and Ed for nearly ten years.

"It's okay. Kyesha's death impacted a lot of people. I've had people watch the documentary—seeing Ed's, Axel's, and my pain—and decided they needed to get clean. I mean, an addict has to do it for themselves...but understanding the impact their illness has on others can be profound. Some good has come out of that documentary." He rubbed his forehead. "Like marrying the bass player..."

Creed snorted. "Well, nothing like banging a rock star."

I glared. "I'd like to think Spencer is with me for my witty personality, sense of humor, and hot body."

This time, Thornton snorted.

I mock glared.

"I think he's with you because he loves you." He winked. "Lion's Gate Bridge and all."

"Oh, good one." Creed nodded vigorously. "You do have a lot in common with Spencer. You've always cared about that environmental shit. And about social justice."

Thornton cocked his head. "What do you care about?"

"Getting laid." Creed headed to the fridge to grab a soda.

"How's that going for you?" The documentarian arched an eyebrow.

I coughed my laugh.

Freddie, who'd been busy scrolling on his phone, snickered.

I elbowed him in the ribs.

He just kept grinning.

Creed waved his hand in disgust and moved up to the front of the bus so he could keep Vera company.

Reese rolled out of her bunk. "Did I hear we're almost here?" She yawned. "I can't believe how long I slept." She slapped my shoulder. "I'll never sleep tonight."

"You will." My phone buzzed with an incoming text, but I ignored it. "We've got rehearsal this evening and our performance tomorrow night. You'll be exhausted by the time we've run through our set. And you'll sleep tonight because you'll want to be at your best tomorrow."

"You promise you won't make noise knocking boots with your boyfriend? Oh, oops, fiancé?"

"We've got a tent. Not that you needed to know that. And we'll be sleeping, I promise." In truth, we hadn't spent a night apart since

I'd returned from Greece. This mini-tour, amazing as it had been, had been hard on my heart.

"I'm going to watch the shred off." Reese grinned. "Give me something to keep me out of trouble. Oh, and the drum-off, of course."

"Of course." I murmured the words. Because where else would our drummer abscond to?

"Meg's participating this year. Which is kinda cool given she gave birth just a few months ago." Thornton checked his phone. "They just hit the Oregon/California border."

"Weren't you from Oregon?" Since he was checking his phone, I felt free to check mine.

"Yep. Then I met a Canadian lad, fell in love, and married him. I'm in the process of obtaining my citizenship. Quite a rigmarole. Totally worth it, though."

"Fair enough. I'm lucky Spencer and I are only from different neighborhoods and not different countries."

"Yes, there is that. Axel and Hugo are much the same. Happy to have overcome their differences."

I chuckled. "That's an interesting story."

"Yep." He glanced out the front windshield.

—*We're in the air.* —

I breathed a sigh of relief.

—*Just get here safely, baby. That's all I want.* —

The rest would sort itself out.

Chapter Twenty-Seven

Spencer

"How are you not nervous?" I tapped my foot to the rhythm of the band on stage currently.

Mama rolled her eyes. "How do you know I'm not nervous?"

"Because I *know* you." And I did. The past year I'd spent a fair amount of time in the woman's company. I felt like she was more of a mother to me than my own. Certainly she filled that role in Malik's life.

And I loved her for it.

We stood near the back of the crowd. In the middle of it, Mama wouldn't have been able to see. Too close to the stage and I worried she might get jostled. She might be a hearty and healthy woman, but she was also on the delicate side, and I worried about her all the time.

She'd hate me if she was aware.

Instead, I said I wanted to be far enough away so I didn't distract Malik.

Mostly bullshit.

In truth, I didn't want to be a distraction. I also wanted to see the entire stage. Pauletta had let me know they had quite a production set up including a film of sorts being projected behind the band.

I was intrigued.

Creed strummed the first few notes of a song I didn't recognize.

The entire group steadfastly refused to share a few of their new songs with us. If I'd attended any of the concerts in the past two weeks, I might've heard some of them. I was dealing with some tricky legislation, though, and hadn't been able to take the time away. Even being here was a pain in my ass, and I had more paperwork to look at before the weekend was over.

Mama elbowed me in the ribs.

"Hey." I scowled.

She pointed to the stage.

Malik stared right at us. Almost like his gaze had been magnetically drawn to me.

He sang a heavy metal song about the pain of unrequited love.

Although I was fascinated to watch him, Creed pulled my attention. Something in the way he played his guitar...it felt authentic. Pain-filled.

"Oh, my dear boy." Mama's words came to me almost as a whisper. Miraculous I could hear them with the deafening sound around us.

"Will he talk to you?" I shouted the words in her ear.

She shook her head. Then shrugged. "It's Creed—who knows what he'll do."

That was true. He could be as hardheaded as Malik when he wanted to be.

The song ended, and they transitioned into one of their classic head-banging rock songs.

Mama bopped to the beat.

I was pretty hopeless, so I just sort of swayed. A white dude with zero rhythm. *And how'd you wind up with a musician exactly? Oh, right, he chained himself to a bridge in the name of the organization you hold so dear. Right. Almost forgot that little tidbit.*

In truth, the year had flown by. Exactly a year ago, he'd stood in my office and pled his case. Or, perhaps more accurately, demanded I allow him to do more. Then the confrontation at city hall, the epic kiss, the quiet meeting of the minds, him coming to my condo...meeting Moses and making sweet love to me. All of that felt like yesterday while also feeling like a million years ago. All those months apart had given time a weird, elastic quality. When I focused on the fact we had the rest of our lives together, things felt more manageable.

Or so I told myself.

"Okay, happy to be here, folks." Malik grinned.

The crowd roared its approval. Almost sixty thousand people made a hell of a ruckus.

"Let me introduce my bandmates." In turn, he said each one's name, and they strummed, keyboarded, or drummed their appreciation. "And I'm Malik. Lead singer and guitarist."

Another roar.

"But I have a secret to share."

My interest piqued.

He put his electric guitar on a stand and bent. When he straightened, he had a violin on his shoulder. With a plug in it and a cable running down to an amplifier.

"Oh my God." My breath caught.

Mama squealed.

Yep. Squealed. Genuine excitement—more than she'd ever shown.

"Have you ever heard him play?"

She shook her head. "He's always kept these two parts of his life separate—before he left the orchestra and after. Maybe he's going to meld the two?"

Such a profound idea, that I found myself leaning forward.

He pulled the bow across the strings just once.

A silence came over the crowd as everyone hushed.

"Some of you may know, I'm an environmentalist."

A few cheers went up.

"Yeah, I even chained myself to a bridge during rush-hour traffic to make a point. I'll say now, that wasn't my brightest move."

"You looked sexy doing it." A woman's voice rang out clear as day.

Everyone laughed.

He saluted her. "True. I always look good."

A few women—and more than a few men—cheered their approval.

"Then I met a man who showed me another way to make a difference. A couple of ways, in fact. One is music. We composed this song for him. Well, and his organization—fighting for change in all the right ways." He met my gaze. "I love you, Spencer. And this is for Pike."

My heart caught in my throat, and I blinked rapidly.

Not rapidly enough. The tears fell unheeded down my cheeks as Malik began playing on his violin. A song I'd never heard before.

Creed's voice carried the tune. A montage of nature shots filled the screen behind them, and the lyrics appeared in bright white.

Words about preserving nature.

About Indigenous rights.

About what it meant to be stewards and keepers of the land.

The lyrics washed over me as the song burrowed into my chest. We'd only spoken of Pike that one night—the winter solstice. Although I held my friend close in my heart, I never spoke of him. The pain was too raw. My own guilt at my own inaction too real.

Somehow, through this song, Mallik was alleviating the guilt. Showing me that I could still do good work—even if my friend was no longer here.

At the end of the song, the crowd erupted into massive cheers.

Malik took a bow, then approached the microphone. "I was trained in classical music. I've learned in the past year that classical and rock music can coexist. Just like humans and nature can coexist. Just like I can coexist with the love of my life." He met my gaze. "It's all a matter of compromise and degrees. Sometimes you have to sit back and let nature take over. We're here on her good graces, of course. We have to respect her. Do our best to care for her. For each other."

"Woo-hoo." Another female voice rang out in the crowd.

He saluted her. "Now, for our finale."

Reese pounded a beat and soon everyone joined in.

They rocked the house down.

Chapter Twenty-Eight

Malik

I mopped my face with a towel Pauletta handed me.

Although I carried my violin case, the road crew, as well as the Rocktoberfest stagehands, cleared our stuff from the stage.

Creed slapped me on the back.

Hard.

"Dude." I coughed.

"Sorry, not sorry." He grinned. "You hit it right out of the park. I don't know who Pike is, but you should've seen your man's face."

I hadn't looked. If I'd met Spencer's gaze in that moment, I might've broken. Because he'd either be moved by my tribute or he'd be pissed as hell—neither reaction could I have borne in that moment.

"They were eating out of the palm of your hand." Pauletta's grin encompassed her entire lovely face. "I'd say that time overseas was worth it."

Much as I would've loved to take credit for the violin idea, that had been Carson. Making it work, however? That was on me.

Reese guzzled her water.

Then noticed Lydia holding the camera pointing right at her.

My drummer gazed toward me and winced.

I shrugged. Given the documentary was going to be a short thirty-minute thing, I doubt one of us chugging hydration ranked in the list of *must have* scenes.

Mickey waved me over. "Found these two just beyond the security perimeter. I managed to get them in."

Mama strode over to Creed while Spencer hesitantly approached me.

I grinned. "It's okay. You're not going to get in trouble."

"Are you sure?" He glanced around, almost as if expecting a security guard to grab him at any moment.

Heedless of my sweaty body, I dragged him in for a hug. He was still here. So I assumed that meant he wasn't pissed about my bringing Pike into the concert.

He pulled back and met my gaze. His eyes were red-rimmed.

"Oh baby, I'm sorry."

"You should be." Mama wagged her finger at me. "Making your beautiful man cry."

"Cry?" Pauletta's focus zeroed in on Spencer.

"Nothing that needs to be shared here." I gestured with my chin to Lydia.

Thornton, who stood off to the side, snickered. "You think Mickey's not going to figure it out?"

Mickey, for their part, merely grinned.

Or Thornton might. He was, after all, the executive producer. And a damn smart man to boot. He'd gotten his start filming nature photography. After his sister's death, he'd moved into *gotcha* journalism.

Why Ed ever trusted the man, I didn't know.

Oh, wait. I wracked my brain. Pauletta took credit for allowing the crew to film Grindstone at their inaugural concert here two years ago. She hadn't known Thornton's connection to the young woman who had died ten years earlier. Or how hellbent he'd been on destroying Ed and Axel.

Now he was married to one of them.

Go figure.

I took a breath.

Spencer, however, put his hand on my chest. "I'll talk about Pike. Just...not here. Not now."

Thornton nodded. "Sure. When you think the moment's right."

I wanted to say *never*, but the decision was Spencer's. If he wanted to talk about his friend—and why he'd chosen activism after that friend died—then that was his choice.

"You need to move along." One of the stagehands gestured for us to leave.

Spencer clung to me as we headed out to the back.

Cool air hit my heated skin. Days were hot in Nevada, even in October, but the nights could cool quickly.

The first notes from the next band reverberated, and the crowd roared.

"They were loud." Freddie grinned. "Seriously. I've never seen a crowd that enthusiastic."

"Possibly because that's the best we've ever played?" Creed held his mother's hand. "All for you, Mama."

She pressed her hand to his cheek. "One day, you'll tell me the truth."

He blinked.

Completely discomposed.

I'd warned him. I'd said that the audience would know. If not the audience, then at least Mama.

Being right brought little vindication as I watched my best friend grin with a smile that didn't reach his eyes. "All good, Mama. I don't know what you're talking about."

She scowled.

"Are we getting food? I'm starving." Freddie pressed a hand to his gut. He could never eat before a gig and so was always ravenous afterward.

"Grindstone has invited you back to their bus. It'll be a tight squeeze, but they want to celebrate your debut." Thornton grinned. "They make the best lasagna—one meat and one vegetarian."

I moaned. "No meat?"

Spencer clasped my hand. "Don't go vegetarian on my account." He pressed a kiss to my cheek. "I love you just the way you are."

"Please tell them we accept their offer." Belatedly I realized I was speaking for a large group of people. I met each of their gazes and all I got back was grins.

"I'll text them." Thornton grabbed his phone out of his back pocket and headed away.

"We're going to be crammed in that bus." Reese shrugged. "Life of a rock star, right?"

"I don't have to go." Mama met my gaze.

"I'm pretty certain we can fit you in." I was so *not* going to point out how tiny she was.

Creed offered me a smile. He mouthed *thank you*.

I smiled my response.

As we were wending our way through the crowd, I grabbed Spencer's arm. "Oh God, isn't that Jameson Crow from Corvus Rising?" I pointed to the tall, solidly built man. His long, dark hair was tied back, and I would've recognized that profile anywhere.

Spencer chuckled quietly. "Did you seriously just ask me that question?"

By the time his meaning sank in, Jameson had melted back into the crowd. "Okay, if I can find him later, I'm going to—"

"Ask him for an autograph?" Spencer clutched my hand as we followed the rather-tall Thornton through the crowd.

"Maybe ask him about his vocals. He and Val are amazing."

"That's fair. Of course, I've never heard of Corvus Rising."

"You need an education on all things rock'n'roll."

"Only if you're the one teaching me. My ears are still ringing."

He really should've been wearing earplugs.

Hopefully Mama had.

Oh God, I'm worrying about hearing loss.

Who knew I'd be all grown up at twenty-eight?

Axel greeted us at the door of the bus and beckoned us in.

Yes, the fit with two bands, husbands, fiancés, a baby, and Mama was tight.

Celebratory and jovial were the two words I'd use. Grindstone toasted our success—with sparkling apple cider—and Pauletta made predictions about our future prospects.

As we ate the most delicious lasagna, she reported on the number of sales of our new album, dropped just over an hour ago.

Numbers that staggered me and far exceeded sales of our last album.

Spencer nuzzled my ear. "I'm so fucking proud of you."

I turned to give him a quick, hard kiss. "Worth the time apart?"

"Completely."

"No nookie." Mama shook her fork at us.

Spencer wrapped his arm around my shoulder.

I leaned into his touch. Even after being home for several months, I never could get enough of it.

"We'll save it for the tent." My fiancé grinned.

"You two need to marry."

I blinked at Mama as I stilled. We'd never discussed a date. After my wonky, awkward proposal, the band had been so focused on to-day—tonight, specifically—that we'd never really discussed *a date*.

"I'd marry him tonight if I could." He tightened his grip on my shoulder.

"You could drive to Reno. Or Vegas." Axel grinned. "As long as you're back to watch our show tomorrow night."

"Sounds...possible." Spencer gazed at me.

I shook my head. "Family and friends. Small and intimate—but family and friends."

"We're not all dragging our butts to Vegas." Meg held her baby tight.

Although Vera, our bus driver, had offered to watch little Ella when Grindstone rehearsed, and then played, Mama insisted she do it.

Vera didn't appear the least bit offended.

To practice for when you all give me grandbabies.

She'd said that directed at me, Spencer, Reese, Freddie and—most especially—Creed.

I would've sworn he'd gone pale.

He was thirty-three and, to my knowledge, had no plans to settle down. Wasn't even seeing anyone seriously.

His younger sister, Abrianna, was still pursuing her PhD and showed no signs of slowing down as she plowed toward academia.

I glanced over to Spencer. He was pale. "Migraine?" I whispered the word.

He shook his head. "I took my preventative pill earlier. It's working. This new drug is amazing." He'd only had a handful of crippling migraines since I'd gotten home. His doctor had gone out on a limb, prescribing an off-label use for an older drug. The medication hadn't initially been created to treat migraines, but that had been an unexpected side effect. Since the risks were minimal, Spencer had been willing to try. Six months of significant relief made the gamble pay off. Whether he'd need to take them for the rest of his life was a question for another day.

Mama eyed him.

He nodded.

Apparently satisfied, she put the last mouthful of lasagna on her fork. "You'll marry at Christmas. I'm organizing. You just have to show up looking respectable." She popped the food into her mouth.

Creed hooted.

I glared. "You're next, my friend."

Again, he desisted immediately.

Okay, something is really wrong.

At that moment, baby Ella started fussing.

"Hand her over." Mama pushed her tray toward me and opened her arms to the baby.

Meg, who was still eating, frowned. "She's been fed."

"Too much noise." Mama took the baby and headed toward the back of the bus.

Big Mac made to rise.

Creed gestured for him to sit back down. "Your daughter couldn't be in better hands."

"And if Mama gets the grandmothering out of her system for a bit, that gives you a reprieve." Spencer turned his attention to my drummer. "I see you."

But he didn't. As perceptive as Spencer could be—and he was fucking good at reading people—he was totally missing Creed's evident pain.

"I need some air." Creed collected a bunch of dishes and carried them to the kitchen.

"Remember we eat ice cream after our show tomorrow night. You're expected to be here." Songbird grinned. "You're our new besties."

Creed waved, then headed out.

Spencer gazed at me.

I nodded. "Yeah, we should be going as well."

"Happy nookie." Pauletta leaned against Mickey. "And we'll head out as well."

They'd head to the camper van while Spencer and I headed to our tent. Not the most glamorous way to hunker down, but I didn't want to be making out on our tour bus with all my nosy bandmates within hearing distance.

Spencer slid off the bench first. He held out his hand and shook hands with each member of Grindstone.

Ed cocked his head.

"You were the inspiration. If Malik hadn't had Black Rock in his sights—knowing you all had made it not once, but twice—who knows where he'd be right now?"

"Possibly in jail." Freddie grinned. "With Mama having to bail him out."

"I heard that." Mama's voice carried from the back of the bus.

"Oh shit." He mumbled that. "I better go before I say anything else that will get me in trouble. Thanks, eh?"

He and Reese rose as well.

En masse, we departed.

Reese and Freddie headed to our bus. As they got in, I couldn't spot Creed. *I hope he's gone to bed and isn't getting into any trouble.* I might have the reputation as the one who did things without thinking about the consequences—but Creed was a close second. Only the idea of disappointing Mama kept him from following some of his more-reckless impulses.

Spencer and I stopped by the tent to grab our toothbrushes. We took super quick showers, brushed our teeth, pissed, and then headed back to our tent.

I sat cross-legged as I sorted out my hair.

He sat on our sleeping bags, eyeing me.

"What?"

"A Christmas wedding?"

I fought with a particularly annoying tangle. "We don't *have* to do what Mama wants."

He arched an eyebrow, visible in the low light. His hair shone a shade darker as he towel dried it.

"Well, if you have your heart set on something else—"

"I don't. I like Mama's suggestion. I don't want you to feel pressured."

"Sweetheart." I grinned. "I proposed to you, remember? The intention was always to, you know, get married. I just wanted to get through the concert first."

"You were amazing."

"Yeah, I kind of was. We all were."

"And now you're going to want to be the face of This Land is Ours."

"Yeah, I kind of do."

He pursed his lips. "All right. You can be the spokesperson if—"

I leaned forward.

"—if you tone it down a little. There's no reason why I can't try my way and your way at the same time. Just no arrests, please?"

I grinned. "Deal."

Epilogue

Spencer

"How, precisely, did we wind up with so many children at our wedding?" I glanced around the room and tried to count.

Meg and Big Mac had brought a very vocal Ella. Her pipes were going to rival Axel's.

Axel and Hugo were fostering two teenagers from Hugo's school. The parents of the twin girls had died a month ago. Rather than letting the girls go into the system, Hugo had stepped up. He wasn't the girls' teacher, so there wasn't any conflict. With the economy being so tight these days, a lot of kids were in the foster system.

The social worker, after performing an extensive home visit, had decided Hugo and Axel would make good foster parents. This hadn't been in their plan, but they'd pivoted beautifully. The two girls often had sad expressions on their faces—totally understandable—but they were smiling today.

Possibly because they'd been tacitly put in charge of Yardley and Johnnie's three foster children. The men were helping out a single mom who was going through a rough patch.

Somehow, through Hugo, Mama had met Yardley—who taught with Hugo—and Johnnie, a hooker for the Vancouver Orcas rugby team. The husbands had been hoping to have kids of their own some-day, and fostering was perfect for them.

Mama had taken the men under her wing. A wing that encom-passed a few other kids I didn't recognize. She'd rented out a hall, and so we had about forty adults and what felt like almost as many children.

"There are so many kids because we let Mama have her way."

"Oh yeah." I grinned. "Good thing—this might've been a boring party without such...entertainment."

"Keeps the rock stars in line. Hard to be the star of the show when you've got a six-year-old girl stealing the microphone and singing her heart out."

I met Malik's gaze. "She's going to be a powerhouse."

"Last year, at Rocktoberfest, one of Hugo's prodigy students sang with Axel."

"If you're still doing this in ten years, I suspect you can look up that..." I frowned. "To whom does she belong?"

"One of Mama's exonerated legal-aid clients."

"Ah, right." Because of course the little one did. Mama's list went far beyond close family and friends. "Hey, where's Creed?"

Malik swiveled his head. "Gone again. He was a great best man, but he's been MIA since the speeches. What do you think that's about?"

"I just don't know. Maybe in the new year you can have a chat with him?"

My husband scoffed. "You think he'll open up to me?" He eyed Mama and Abrianna. "I think even they're in the dark."

"Maybe I'm making too much of this." I sipped my hot chocolate—the drink we'd served instead of champagne. Well, and eggnog—but that shit was just gross.

Reese drank it by the cartonful.

I'd always wondered about her.

Ah, aside from her enjoyment of weird Christmas beverages, she was a good woman. Every single person here was the best. They'd made today special—if a little eccentric.

"You ready to dance?" Malik rose and held out his hand.

"To our forever?"

He grinned. "You better believe it."

And so we did.

Miss out on a previous season? Ed and Thornton's story is told in Axe to Grind (Road to Rocktoberfest 2023). Axel and Hugo's story is in Grindstone's Edge (Road to Rocktoberfest 2024)

Creed's story is coming October 2026!

Want more Gabbi Grey?

Check out her Love in Mission City series, set in beautiful British Columbia.

The first book is

Ginger Snapping All the Way (Love in Mission City Book 1)

Also available:

Stanley's Christmas Redemption (Love in Mission City Book 2)
The Beauty of the Beast (Love in Mission City Book 2.5)
Sleigh Bells and Second Chances (Love in Mission City Book 3)
A Daddy for Christmas 2: Foster (Love in Mission City Book 3.5)
Rayne's Return (Love in Mission City Book 4)
Gideon's Gratitude (Love in Mission City Book 5)
Quinton's Quest (Love in Mission City Book 6)
Love in Mission City: The Boyfriend Gamble
Love in Mission City: The Four Seasons
Love in Mission City: The Boyfriends Duet
Love in Mission City: The Shorts
Rayne Check
Archer's Awakening
Leo's Lust
Finn's Find
A Daddy for Christmas 3: Lorcan
Thought You Were the One
Love Without Reservations
Page Against the Machine
The Lightkeeper's Love Affair
Ace's Place
Marcus's Cadence

Not in it for the Money

Also:

Axe to Grind (Road to Rocktoberfest 2023)

Grindstone's Edge (Road to Rocktoberfest 2024)

Voice to Raise (Road to Rocktoberfest 2025)

Hugh (Single Dads of Gaynor Beach)

Anthony (Single Dads of Gaynor Beach)

Xavier (Single Dads of Gaynor Beach)

Love Furever (Friends of Gaynor Beach Animal Rescue)

Husky Love (Friends of Gaynor Beach Animal Rescue)

Yorkie to My Heart (Friends of Gaynor Beach Animal Rescue)

A Furever Home (co-written with Kaje Harper – Friends of Gaynor
Beach Animal Rescue)

My Past, Your Future

If Only for Today

Catch a Tiger by the Tail

Solstice Surprise

Valentino in Vancouver

You See Me

Sun, Surf, and Surprises

Ginger in the City

Caressa's Homecoming (Bound by Love Book 1)

Cole's Reckoning (Bound by Love Book 2)

An Uncommon Gentleman

A Sensible Gentleman

A Wounded Gentleman

Didn't See You Coming

Finding Noah (Foggy Basin Season 2)

Noah's Holiday (A Foggy Basin Short Story)

Hot Rucking Canadian

Big Rucking Disaster

Unlocked and Unlost

Audiobooks

Ginger Snapping All the Way

Stanley's Christmas Redemption

Sleigh Bells and Second Chances

Rayne's Return

Gideon's Gratitude

Quinton's Quest

Rayne Check

Archer's Awakening

Leo's Lust

Thought You Were the One

Love in Mission City: The Shorts

Page Against the Machine

The Lightkeeper's Love Affair

Ace's Place

Marcus's Cadence

Not in it for the Money

Hugh (Single Dads of Gaynor Beach)

Anthony (Single Dads of Gaynor Beach)

Love Furever (Friends of Gaynor Beach Animal Rescue)

Husky Love (Friends of Gaynor Beach Animal Rescue)

A Furever Home (co-written with Kaje Harper – Friends of Gaynor
Beach Animal Rescue)
My Past, Your Future
If Only for Today
Catch a Tiger by the Tail
Solstice Surprise
An Uncommon Gentleman
A Sensible Gentleman
Didn't See You Coming

Want a free short story? The story is set in Gaynor Beach, California
where there are plenty of single dads and puppy rescues! You can sign
up for my newsletter so you can keep up with all the great stuff I'm
doing as well as pictures of my own pooches, Ally and Finnegan.

Hemingway's Happy Day

Love contemporary MF romances? What's better than love in the
beautiful Cedar Valley in British Columbia, Canada? Find small town
romances with a touch of angst, a bit of heat, and a lot of heart...

The Absolution of Abigail Reardon (prequel)
The Luminosity of Loriana Harper (Book 1)
The Making of Marnie Jones (Book 2)
The Redemption of Remy St. Claire (Book 3)

Interested in knowing more about Gabbi?

Sign up for her newsletter
, Follow her on Bookbub
Follow her on Instagram

USA Today Bestselling author Gabbi Grey lives in beautiful British Columbia where her fur baby chin-poo keeps her safe from the nasty neighborhood squirrels. Working for the government by day, she spends her early mornings writing contemporary, gay, sweet, and dark erotic BDSM romances. While she firmly believes in happy endings, she also believes in making her characters suffer before finding their true love. She also writes m/f romances as Gabbi Black and Gabbi Powell.